A Bloody Good Massacre

By

David Scott

Teddy was here

BOOK TITLE

VI Publication

davidscottwrites@gmail.com

ISBN: 978-1-7396154-0-6

Foreward

By

Adam Kelly, the editor of A Bloody
Good Massacre

This book is a love letter, one of darkness and depravity with glimmers of decency.

It comes from a good heart swayed by glorious violence.

Prologue to a Massacre

He was not alone here. Slowly he walked through the vast frigid room while the industrial coolers hummed constantly above him. Surrounding him were walls of black black mesh, LEDs glittering behind it; the computer servers for this year's event that would make broadcasting to a worldwide audience possible. He placed his shaking hand onto one of them feeling it hum and warmth beneath his touch.

 "It's almost time." He said to the man standing silently behind him, he was his junior by nearly forty years.

 The younger man smiled and brushed his hand through his prematurely grey hair, "It will be a record breaker. I feel it in my bones."

The old man turned to him and eyed him warningly, "There's plenty of room for clusterfuck if mishandled, minimum length to the event should be three days… I've seen it end in hours. This venue is troublesome."

  The other man threw his hands up in mock defense, "I've been personally overseeing the set up for this event. We've done a major overhaul on the tech. New cameras, microphones, trackers and hell, we even have drones this year." He counted off the points on his long thin fingers.

"Hoping to make it a true spectacle."

"You've seen our choices for the roster."
The old man cleared his throat, "Mostly cannon fodder but a good handful of crowd pleasers. No legends though."
The young man shook his head, "Not many wanting or willing to return no matter the size of the pay cheque, though I did manage to get your favourite… He was a late entry so may not get into the roster on time, though if we have any drop outs he's first in."

Slowly the old man nodded, "How did you find him?"

"He called us," the younger man placed his hand onto the elder's shoulder "He said he'd have gotten to us sooner but mixed up the dates."

"Christ he's been a oddity since day one." shrugging the hand away he began to stride towards the exit, "See that you do not screw up your new position Mr Director, the executives are always wary of new blood."

The Director smiled slowly, "I'll do my best and good luck to you" he eyed him with care "Mister Producer."

Chapter one: Ticking Clock

The drugs were hitting Victoria hard.

Between the bouts of psychedelic lucidity in other realms were brief, painful moments of uncontrollable reality. The inescapable nightmare was chaotic and fluid, shifting between coherent thought and horrid imagination. Peeling back the eyelids, the blinkers and the intentional oversights before piercing to the point where all the forgotten memories lay hidden away. Tearing them out despite your kicking and screaming, bringing them into the harsh perception of waking, honest thought.

Once she'd briefly woke to see lights wash past her vision as she was wheeled down a corridor by two individuals who could be doctors, before crashing back into the wash of flashing horrors and molten colours. The long buried memories slid through the filmy membrane of her subconscious. She did not know what she was remembering. A party moved around her. Before her was a cake with three candles. It was a birthday. It was not hers.

A sting in her arm brought her back to painful lucidity. She watched as one of them pulled a thin needle from her arm.

He leaned in; a medical mask covered most of his face only revealing two dark glassy eyes, "Well now. I hope you enjoy yourself."

Darkness descended with an unresolving, final click. Two sets of footsteps left her alone, echoing away into the void. Some distance away the sound of a heavy metal door closing made its way to her. Victoria did not let panic set in. She kept her breathing slow, centered and did not let fear win. Victoria was seated, held by her wrists and ankles by steel shackles. The fog of the drugs was fading fast, her keen senses returned slowly and her vision adjusted to the dark. She was in a small room; her chair was in the centre of it. Before her was a large rectangle.

"It will be a TV." She said to herself. "Have to set the ground rules somehow."

Victoria settled back into the chair and began to enjoy the feeling of somewhat complete mental capacity after her drug trip.

She was not a victim.

She'd not been kidnapped.

She'd gone willingly.

She'd fought to be here.

She had no regrets.

The small red light foreshadowed great discomfort. The television exploded into crackling static, blinding her momentarily.

"Fuck." The curse crept from her mouth as she forced her eyes open to look at the screen. The screen was entirely black except for four shifting red digits.

10:00

Even as she watched the ticking clock, she could still feel how heavy her eyes where, the drugs had left a heavy fog upon her.

09:04

She shook her head ignoring the grating feeling of what was lost. She only knew the timer.

08:32

Seconds ticking away before it began.

07:45

The sweat that began on her neck was now trickling between her shoulder blades.

06:27

"They are trying to wind us up. Make us lash out."

04: 57

The countdown shrunk down to the bottom right hand corner of the screen as a man with grey hair, tanned skin and an expensive suit smiled back at her with the most perfectly pearl white teeth.

Through his shark like smile he began, "Well first and foremost I would like to thank you all for entering this year's Massacre. I am the Director of the proceedings. Like Gladiators of old, you are about to enter the Amphitheater where the masses will watch you and find glorious entertainment in your display.

Now for where our Amphitheater is located." A map popped up in the lower left-hand corner of the screen, it was of the United Kingdom and Ireland. A small red dot off the southern coast of Ireland appeared, "You are here. Here is the island of Cuimilt Dé, it's not too big. It could hold an approximate population of thirty-three thousand people. Right now, it's got a surprisingly grand, rather select total of forty-five. That's you and forty-four other morally dubious individuals who all wish to compete for the money.

As you all know from previous years, the prize fund is sitting pretty at one hundred and twenty five million pounds sterling."

The silver haired man's smile somehow, almost impossibly managed to widen, "To get this you simply need to be the last surviving soul on this island. Kill or be killed. For every of these individuals you kill, you receive a bonus of five hundred thousand pounds. If you lose, all the bonuses that you acquire go to whomever you name to be your next of kin.

Now we are reaching the final minutes of our countdown…"

02:45

"… so let me tell you what we've got for you. Once you are released from your bonds you will find a bag behind your chair. Inside is your weapon of choice, sorry for all you gun nuts - no ammo - but we've left enough scattered around your playground, as well as delivering regular ammo drops throughout the Massacre and bringing in the really spectacular stuff when we are on the home stretch."

02:22

"Only one rule is in place. *Do not try to escape the Massacre.* A bounty will automatically be placed onto your person, in that case, no stone will be left unturned, no corner of the earth won't be searched, you will be brought back for punishment."

His face became angry as a seemingly still image appeared in the screen.

Victoria wretched and looked away from the picture of what had once been a human being.

Its limbs were gone, replaced with bloodied stumps, between its legs was a sexless mound of stitching, its face was missing its nose, eyelids and most of its lower jaw leaving a horrid twisted open hole down its throat while it looked unblinkingly at the ceiling.

From every crevice and hole tubes and wires snaked around its body running back into a life support machine.

01:58

The Director reappeared emotionless, "That was last year's dropout Michael Gardner. For those wondering, yes, he is still very much alive and no, he does not want to be. Customary with dropout rules he will be euthanised the moment the countdown ends, much to his relief I imagine."

01:20

That original smile with the impossibly white teeth came back with vigour, "This year's broadcast will hit over one hundred countries and the many cameras around the island will capture the onslaught of carnage. So please be creative with how you kill your fellow competitors. We get all kinds watching." He winked cheekily.

00:45

"Now in my closing statement before we let you all loose, just try to remember there is an awfully high possibility that you will die, so do please try to enjoy your last moments in that case, perhaps taking the life that wanted your own."

He suddenly perked up as someone handed him a piece of paper from off camera, an eyebrow raised as he read "We've just got word that we have a late entry replacing someone who is unfortunately too ill to compete, it is the one and only three time returning champion Teddy. I must say he is a personal favourite of ours and I cannot wait to see what he's got in store for all of you."

00:08

"Good Night and God Bless."

00:00

The television snapped in to darkness, back to the empty, black rectangle as the metal cuffs around Victoria's wrists and ankles let loose in symphony with the lights of the room erupting, another blinding moment.

She spun reaching behind the chair and feeling for the bag. Taking it, she pulled it onto her lap.

Inside was a long, serrated Bowie knife complete with a thoroughly worn in leather sheath. Underneath it was an old brown leather flight jacket. She pulled on the old coat and slipped her belt through the sheath, flung the bag over her shoulder and bolted towards the door. It led to a long dark corridor with a single door at the far end. The door was heavy steel, she had to put her back into budging it at all, as she pushed, she felt the rush of fragrant, hot summer's air hit her face and her eyes burned with the sun gleaming into the dimly lit hall.

She pushed harder and the door gave way causing her to slip and fall onto grass. The heat of the sun hit her as she stood looking. Victoria was on one side of a valley coming out of a rolling green hill. There she looked down, and in the valley was a town beside the sea. Within the town Victoria could see a suburban area, high street and a dock area with warehouses.

She thought to herself, "The smart bet would be that most of the competitors would head towards it while others would head upwards to safety, but there would probably be supplies down there. Food, water, weapons. It would be dangerous to be sure, but I could get something if I am quick and avoid the others tonight, as most would wait for darkness to approach." Her options stood before her. Be smart and safe or be reckless and gamble.

She started to make her way towards the town. Every step her hand was on the handle of the blade on her belt tucked under her jacket.

Across the island more doors opened and out stepped her hunters and victims.

Victoria was thankful her descent was mostly in cover provided by a smattering of sturdy old trees. She knew she was bound to run into another player eventually. She'd been warned by her handler that some of them were true freaks.

Psychos, maniacs, cannibals, sociopaths, rapists, sadists, pyromaniacs, thugs and assassins. The list went on and on. Every twisted variation of killer could be found here.

She knew this as she wasn't just one of them, she was one of the worst. Judgement wasn't hers to cast, though her peers were all would-be executioners.

Some doors opened, some were more difficult but these monsters were let loose. In one room a pallid creature crept out the door, knives in hand, another whistled a jaunty tune.

Chapter two: First Blood

Victoria vaulted the fence and landed in a mostly empty car park behind a shopping centre. Every car there was a hollow shell, no engines only hollow spaces beneath their bonnets.

"Everything is for show." She muttered to herself.

She crept between the rows of cars getting closer and closer to the half open shutter at the back of the shopping centre. Victoria rolled under, spotting the broken padlock. She was not the first one here.

Her knife was drawn as she walked into the empty mall. Lights on, shops open and the same bad music from Dawn of the Dead was playing. One soft footstep after the other. In the store fronts she could see everything that any contestant would want. Mannequins posing with bags of food, bottles of water, even a few dressed up as Rambo not to mention the Terminator, all sporting various weapons. All of this behind glass, noisy if broken.

Coming in from the back had been a stroke of luck, convenient but also a question, who else came this way?

She cautiously stepped forward and examined the lifeless caricatures. A swear caught in the back of her throat when she spotted that each was bound to wires.

"Explosives." She thought to herself, "Placed here by a player or the powers that be?"

She didn't dare take one of the more vicious looking machine guns, but she spotted a holster around 'Snake Pliskon's' waist. Slowly Victoria unbuckled and pulled it free, jumping back a few feet as it swung away from the body.

Nothing happened.

She looked over her prize. A small brown leather holster with a snub-nosed Rossi 44. Magnum pistol. Fully loaded with twenty-four bullets handily stored in the holster, though to Victoria's annoyance no silencer.

She strapped it on and felt the weight of the gun against her hip. Victoria slid the knife back into its sheath and brought up her new firearm. The weight of cruel black metal that delivered at a distant was a comfort.

A crash echoed through the mall a cacophony causing her spin with malice, gun ready and tracing through the air to her target. Out of one of the faux store fronts two men crashed out, one brandishing a crowbar the other a sledgehammer.

The man with the crowbar was a tall thin Nigerian, while the man with the hammer was a stocky looking Spaniard. The Spaniard got lucky and the hammer crushed through the Nigerian's knee with a wild swing, one that could've easily missed, dropping him to the ground.

He screamed out in agony as the Spaniard stood over him, hammer raised, hanging for the killing blow.

It came silent, no effort but to swing. The heavy thud was final, mixed with a wet crunch as the front of the man's head met the back.

He slid his hand up the handle ready to pull the bloodied hammer free from the mess of grey matter and gore only to freeze as he saw Victoria training her gun on him.

He opened his mouth.

She pulled the trigger.

A hole was drilled through his head by the piece of lead entering just below his right eye. He stumbled, his mouth moving silently as if to talk, before collapsing back onto the man he'd just killed.

Victoria stood stock still, the sound of the gunshot still ringing in her ears and echoing through the mall.

She breathed out and holstered the gun.

Upon the Spaniard's back was a full bag, she removed it from him.

It had water, rations, a compass, a nice wristwatch and to her surprise, a garrote wire.

"This your's hitman?" She asked.

She checked the Nigerian, but his bag seemed to be missing. Victoria bagged the loot and ran.

Gary entered the town walking slowly down the middle of the street.

His appearance was peculiar to say the least. Platinum blonde hair, white face paint, smiling red mouth painted over his and the tip of his nose painted red.

Here was a killer disguised as a clown. His red suit fitted him well, but looked to be deceptively baggy with his long red coat flowing behind him.

His weapons of choice hung by his side, completely alien to rest of his attire. The two blades where a long Uchigatana sword and a shorter Daishō blade.

"Well you look fucking ridiculous."

Gary turned to the sound of the address, finding a biker sporting a thick moustachedressed in nothing but leather and a black Sabbath t-shirt approaching him. In his hand was a crossbow.

"Go on then." The man laughed, spitting as he spoke, "Tell me a joke."

Gary cocked one of his painted eyebrows, "Well, there's one in front of me from the looks of things."

"What?" More spit catching and clinging to his chin.

"You're shaking. I'm guessing you're an addict of some kind." Gary eased himself with measured steps around the big man.

"What?"

"You're in withdrawal. Whatever they gave us to wake us up must have flushed everything out of your system. Can you even see me clearly right now?"

"Shut up." He kept the bow aimed at the Clown Samurai.

Gary placed his hand slowly onto the grip. "Why did you enter?" still circling his enemy, slowly getting closer.

"The money!"

"Good enough reason." Gary said keeping a firm grip on the Uchigatana.

The ragged twitches said it was time.

"Fuck you!" The man screamed as he pulled the trigger.

Gary did not dodge; he did not flinch and in one single movement he unsheathed his long blade and sliced the arrow out of the air. The moustached assailant's bravado disappeared, he cowered trying to reload the ungainly crossbow. Gary moved quickly, closing on his attacker.

The biker watched the bow and his forearm disappear in to the bloody mist spurting from where they should be.

He had time to think 'where did they go?', he didn't feel the blade cut straight through his neck severing his head from his body.

Gary cleaned the Uchigatana on his sleeve and sheathed it. He continued his slow walk into the town leaving the twitching body behind him without a second thought.

 Victoria was on her way to leave via the back entrance she'd used to enter the mall. Always go out the door you came rang in her head. Whistling coming from the mall behind her. The tune caught in her head.

Pop goes the weasel.

A shiver ran through her spine at the children's song.

 She decided to run.

 The Spaniard and the Nigerian's bodies lay still in the middle of the mall as the whistling grew louder and louder, with faint footsteps coming closer and closer. The last four notes whistled out as the person whistling came to a stop just beside the bodies.

 "Oh, my oh my have I missed the fun?" An expensive brown shoe came down heel first in disapproval, "I was hoping to be the first to kill someone. But look here. You beat his brains out…how rude…I wanted to do that…well no…I'd have set him on fire…I should find someone to set on fire…have myself a barbecue…yes, a barbecue. What a wonderful idea if I don't say so myself. Perfect way to spend this sort of weather."

The man spun on his heels and began to walk away before stopping.

"But oh…" he turned to the bodies, "You killed him but who killed you?" The man pulled the Spaniards head up and looked, "Oh… you managed to get in the way of a bullet… silly ducky." He let the head go and it slapped back down into the puddle of blood and brain tissue. The man huffed, "That means I'm not even the second person to kill someone…oh bother. I'll have to remedy this…I'll have to invite a lot of people to my barbecue and set them all on fire…yes that will do it. Ah fire my faithful old friend, you've not failed me yet."

With a now happy mood the man walked off briskly breaking into song,

"Oh row row row your boat gently down the stream…now that Teddy is on board he'll listen to you scream."

Chapter three: Just Remember

Victoria checked her new watch, quarter to nine in the evening. She was halfway up the hill she'd come down as the sun began to set. Shelter was paramount this evening if she wanted to avoid a cold night beneath the stars, in the open. Across from her, along the valley, she could see lights of fires and torches.

"Wonder how many will die tonight?" She thought as she climbed higher.

Dusk ended and twilight descended as she found herself walking over the crest of the hill and finding a wood before her, tall thin trees rising around her.

The walk turned into a silent jog, the ground soft and thick with pine needles.

The woods were wild and overgrown but the path was clear and well maintained. The wind whistled through the trees, shifting their branches against each other, the only sounds apart from the soft, carefully timed footfalls of the assassin running through the woods.

She stopped in the clearing.

Before her was a small cabin. Gun in hand she approached. It was only one story tall and its windows were boarded up tight, the door looking like it had been nailed back together, the porch swing hung silent, not shifted by the breeze.

Her mind rolled the options around, prying those boards off wouldn't be quiet.

She walked around the cabin, surveying and taking in every possible entrance. Then she spotted it. A loose plank around the base. She took her knife and hammered it in with the heel of her palm, the first attempt at prying it off snapped the tip off. The second bore slowly cracking fruit. Before her was a dark crawlspace beneath the cabin floor. She climbed in and pulled the plank with her closing it tighter than she'd found it. She crawled, barely a foot of head room. Uncomfortably she dragged herself, feeling the dry dirt beneath her and the cobwebs snaking across her face until she found a silhouetted square of light. She pushed it upward but stopping at an inch. She looked through the trap door. It was dark but moonlight had now begun to shine through the boarded-up windows, gently illuminating the cabin.

A stone fireplace, an old leather chair, a musty sofa and a rocking chair in the corner. Above the fireplace was a deer's head frozen in a maniacal laugh.

Victoria sighed heavily realising she'd just snuck into a replica of the cabin from the Evil Dead films. She crept inside.

The Dog was hunting.

That's how he was raised, be a dog. Obey.

That's how he was trained, be a dog. Obey.

That's how he killed, be a dog. Obey.

The giant of a man waded through a river with his club in his hand.

Long, dirty hair clung to his unwashed face, while long rags draped over his hulking form sufficed as clothes.

"Good boy." The voice cooed in his ear. "You know what to do when you find them?"

The Dog's mouth twisted, "I…I…I break them."

"That's a good boy. You break them good." The voice was cruel and the Dog knew this.

"I…I."

"You don't speak unless you're answering a

fucking question of mine mutt!" The voice
sneered.

The Dog went silent.

"Good boy."

The Dog got to the bank and pulled himself
out of the water. He towered over everything at
7"2 with impossibly broad shoulders.
Everything was small compared to him. Even
the trees, trunks looking fine and dainty next to
this brute. He looked into the sky to see the
crescent moon hanging over head. He howled.

Victoria froze as the howl hit her. She could
hear it echoing through the woods. The sound
of an animal.

Slowly she crawled into the bathtub, in the
barely separate bathroom and drew the curtain.
She'd moved a large armchair over the trap
door and placed a vase precariously atop it as a
cheap intruder alarm. She lay back ill at ease,
pulling her folded jacket lower, giving her neck
some cushioning too. It would do as a pillow.

She was not sleeping.

She was resting.

She was recovering.

Victoria could still feel the effects of the drugs in her system. Whatever they'd used to wake her up had not fully banished the drugs that had kept her sedated. She could feel her hands shaking slightly. She couldn't take any chances. Above her in the dark she could see something. Something shining. She forgot about her shaking hands and stood in the bathtub.

Just in the wall, was a tiny glass circle no bigger than the head of a match.

"Camera…"

She gently rubbed the glass and lay back down.

They were always watching, perhaps the audience too.

The thought played in her mind, would she end up as another video clip along with the other doomed players, a part of another twisted snuff-reel. Out there in the world someone was watching her lay in this bathtub holding her gun. For a moment she thought about shooting the voyeuristic camera but beyond the thought of noise, her shaking hands and numb fingers killed the daydream. She stretched out as far as she could to get comfy and made great efforts to let her muscles relax.

The sounds of the shots hit her.

They'd made it to the town.

Gary sat atop the rooftop looking down.

A man lay dead on the street below, a jagged hole puncturing his back, exposing bone, sinew and what was left of his vital organs. Shots rang out inside of the building he was atop of. The clown lay on his back. He'd made it up here via a skylight that he'd bolted shut behind him.

Gary wasn't worried about the gun shots. He just lay looking up at his hand, it still had a slight tremor from the drugs in his system.

Something caught his ear.

Whistling.

The gunshots ceased.

"Get the fuck off of me!" came a woman's scream before a dull thud echoed below him.

Gary slid over to the skylight. The whistling continued. He peered over the ledge slowly. He could see a young man holding a machine gun, it trembled in his hands. The whistling got louder and the lights flickered out. Gary didn't dare move but his hand crept to the long handle of his sword.

A flicker of light and he could see something. A fine blue suit and the back of a large round brown head was all he could see standing behind the young man.

Darkness again.

The whistling stopped.

Light returned and the room was empty.

Gary slowly moved away from the skylight never taking his eyes off of it.

The shaking had spread from his hand to deep in his stomach, his diaphragm twitched, he was barely in charge. The drugs weren't to blame; he'd recognized the song that the creature whistled.

'Baa baa black sheep.'

Chapter Four: Needs some salt

Bungalows, gardens and picket fences.

Haru did not expect to find these on the island. To his knowledge they looked to be from every American suburbia all at once which only confused him more.

Every house had its lights on and street lamps buzzed gently above every 200 yards. He sucked his teeth as he stood surveying his heartless, decorative environment.

To anyone seeing Haru they would make out a Japanese gentleman in his mid-30's with short dark hair, thin trimmed goatee, dressed in an expensive looking black suit. But beneath the suit, hidden away from the casual onlooker were his true colours. Painstakingly scribed tattoos. Starting between his shoulders, covering each arm, around his chest, down his spine and all the way down his legs to his ankles. It had taken four years to get them finished and it had been painful but so very worth it in his opinion. Every line of every character on him could tell a story but only one did not represent a part of him. Dead center of his chest he bore a calm Buddha, his visage projecting nothing but serenity, a beautiful and well considered likeness. At its core, not the man Haru was.

Serenity was a distinct daydream, like all of the others, he'd woken up in a room shackled to a chair and watching a television. Like all of the others, he'd escaped into a long hallway. Unlike the others, his door hadn't opened.

Haru had spent his first two hours of the Massacre prying his door open with one of the arms of his chair.

It had angered him knowing that his elder brother could see him like that.

Trapped.

Scared.

Failing.

He shook it off. He was out now and he was baying for blood.

The Yakuza enforcer sighed; he still couldn't find anyone.

Haru could hear his elder brother's voice in his

head, "Be calm and be patient."

He knew this to be true.

The impotent hours left him frustrated, he decided to go exploring. He took the first bungalow on his left and entered. Upon opening the door, he saw a figure before him. With one motion he drew his pistol and fired only to watch a mannequin collapse down into itself.

Haru looked on mystified, as he could now see that in the living room there was a whole family of them watching the television.

A television showing him standing in a doorway looking confused. He backed away slowly watching his televisual doppelganger do so a second behind him.

He now knew why the suburbia he found himself in unsettled him so.

This town wasn't just faceless suburbia, this was the same town seen turned to ash by nuclear testing. The same town that appeared in countless videos and documentaries being torn apart by a fury only stars match. He began to run, run away from the test town before it burned too. That they were all built off a general plan might have been somewhere in his mind, but not at the forefront.

Victoria's hand had not shaken in half an hour.

She slithered out of the bath knowing that she was still being watched. She pulled her jacket back on and began to walk through the cabin. Victoria perked her ear up. She could hear music. Music that was coming from very far away.

The Dog could hear music as he waded through the bog.

Haru could hear music as he ran from the false town made for doom.

Gary could hear music from his rooftop.

The music carried to every part of the island.

As the sun rose over the horizon, the stack of speakers sitting atop the central peak of the island only increased their song. The song was a bombastic marching song, the liberty bell. Behind the speakers was a tall pyre with a man tied to it, gagged and blindfolded.

He struggled and screamed as the deafening music resonating within his skull. The music ceased, ringing in the ears of those close.. Something splashed over the bound man

He could smell it.

Feel it, the way it flashed off and dried his skin.

Petrol.

His panicked flailing only increased.

"Oh, will you stop that. You're getting it everywhere." his captor said with an annoyed tone.

The petrol-soaked man screamed into his gag.

"What is it?"

The blindfold was ripped from the bound man's head along with the gag.

He looked up half blinded by the sun ready to scream but one look at his captor but that scream died in his throat.

It was not because he held the red plastic petrol can, or for the fact he had a pistol strapped to his hip, or for that he seemed to be wearing a necklace made of human ears.

It was because here stood Teddy.

Teddy wasn't an obvious terror, here stood a well-heeled man with polished shoes in a fine pinstripe suit that fit him well. Winklepickers, that's what they're called, long and pointed – cruel and sleek on the right man. Staring at those shoes was easier.

That well-cut figure was topped by an all too big head, like that of a mascot.

Teddy, so named for good reason gazed upon him with the cheerful face of a child's bear. This was the imaginary friend that slew enemies, charming and graceful but not this man's friend, piss ran down his leg.

"You…you're Teddy?" The terrified man spoke.

Teddy straightened his tie while leaning forward until he was mere inches from his captive's face, "Well yes little ducky and who might you be?"

"I'm Paul."

"Well pleasure to meet you Paul," Teddy shook one of Paul's bound hands, "Now I'm just going to set fire to you."

"What why?!?"

"Why not?"

Paul wept as he pleaded for a less horrible fate, "Please don't set me on fire. Shoot me, stab me, fucking strangle me but for the love of fuck don't set me on fire."

"But," Teddy began while pouring a small trail of petrol away from Paul, "If I don't set you on fire, however will I get my barbecue?"

"Wait…you're going to fucking eat me?!?"

"Not all of you, I'm not greedy."

"That's not fucking comforting!"

Teddy set down the can while tutting loudly, "You do swear a lot Paul, you may want to question how that will appear to people you've only just made friends with. Some may find it rude…even, dare I say, off-putting."

"Fuck you, you sick fucking cunt of a fuck!" cried Paul as he thrashed against his bindings uselessly.

Teddy placed his hands on his hips, "Now Paul, by some may find it rude, I really mean I, personally find rude. There are so many words in the vastness of the English language for you to choose from and you've used, 'and pardon my French', the F word seven times in under forty-five seconds. I see it as a flaw in your character that you may want to think upon."

"How am I going to work on it while I'm dead?"

"Now now, the fire won't kill you for a good three minutes, that's plenty of time to think of your shortcomings as any sort of pleasant human being."

Teddy drew a lighter from his pocket.

He rolled it around in his hand, opened the lid and struck the flint wheel. As the spark hit the wick there was a tiny whoomph.

"I'm sorry…" the terrified man said grasping at straws hoping that he'd find a winner, something that might appeal to the madman with the teddy bear's face.

Teddy hopped forward and stopped an inch from Paul's trembling face with a terrifying speed, "Pardon."

"I'm sorry."

"No." Teddy tapped Paul on the nose with an outstretched finger, "Why are you sorry?"

"I'm sorry I said fuck and insulted you."

Teddy closed the lighter and danced away, "You see, that's very big of you. Shows an ability to grow and from what I've seen, that is a very big step forward for you. Paul, I accept your apology."

Paul smiled.

"But I'm still setting you on fire."

Paul stopped smiling.

Teddy rolled the lighter in his palm once again, opened it and struck a flame, gracefully tilted forward to touch the puddle on the ground with the bare flame.

The whoomph came, by this time it was nearly a thump, given the gallon of petrol Teddy had thrown around. The flames didn't follow the trail, they were just there, consuming Paul, he thrashed and screamed.

Teddy put his music back on and sat down on a folding lawn chair that he'd found after kidnapping Paul. While Paul's screams began to die out as drawing breath to scream brought smoke and flame in to his lungs, Teddy began to sing along with the bombastic marching band.

After a good three minutes Teddy approached the smouldering, cracking corpse and drew a knife. He sliced off a long slither of Paul's blackened cheek with care, plucked it delicately up with his thumb and forefinger then gently slid it under his mask. The sound of chewing and crunching came from within as he tapped his foot.

He lowered his head disapprovingly and tutted, "Needs some salt."

Chapter Five: The director's chair

The Director watched the screens before him.

Sixty-four of them to be exact. 8x8 layout, each showing a different scene.

On screen with #27 Teddy was skinning his latest victim while on #50 Victoria crept out of the cabin's crawl space, while #12 flicked between a multitude of various angles showing Haru's escape from the doomed suburbia.

The Director lounged in his leather chair, feet on a matching stool, he stared at the screens seeming almost blank eyed, taking all of it in.

He pressed a button on his earpiece, "Give us two more minutes on Teddy. The snuff crowd will love it." His face contorted, "Where is Bora?"

The earpiece buzzed and the Editor spoke, "We've a search for him ongoing. We had him at station 14 which brought him up in…"

"The Castle I know. I take it he cut his tracker out."

"He cut it out of his calf and left it in his cell. Used the tip of his machete."

"I don't think those things are machetes," the Director sighed, "How many removed their trackers?"

A moment of silence, "Well Bora, Family Man, Moe, Bloody Mary, Gary and Teddy. Though Teddy put his in his pocket."

The Director watched as Teddy began playing keepie uppie with his burnt victim's severed head like a football, given the state of the head and its weight, not an unimpressive feat.

"Is anyone in combat right now?" he asked while internally counting how long Teddy could keep the head bouncing in the air.

"No but Family Man seems to be gathering people."

"Oh, has he formed a group?" the Director smiled at the idea, "How many has he got so far?"

"Four."

"Four in only the first hours…impressive. How many rejected?"

"None. He does seem to have a way with words."

The Director stood, "Show me."

Four of the centre televisions flicked to form one single image.

In the view was a Caucasian man in his late 50's. Short brown hair, clean shaven, wearing thick framed glasses. Wearing a white shirt with a brown tanned leather jacket.

"When was the last time we had a group?"

"Well it was the Massacre of '02. Group of twelve who managed to make it to the final eighteen before one of them turned."

"Ah the Bruno incident. Did it with a flame thrower if I remember?"

"Petrol bomb, but yes."

The Director cautiously stepped towards the screen, "I wonder how long he can keep these psychopaths in line." He caught a look at the man in the back, "Who is that man at the back wearing the pink shirt?"

"That is 'Patient four.'"

"Ah, doesn't he call himself Jesus?" the Director sat back down, "Well this should be interesting. Keep them on camera the entire time; make sure to send updates to the betting pool. Who is this year's favourite?" He shook his head, "I mean who is below Teddy?"

"Well the Massacre bookies are giving good odds to Bora and Gary though next is Marlow."

The Director shook his head, "Marlow won't come close to winning. He just looks the part, but he's utterly insane."

"On a side note this year's favourite is already dead."

"You mean it wasn't Teddy?"

"No."

"Who was it?"

"He is the man Teddy is currently eating."

He laughed, "Oh nicely done Teddy, nicely done."

The Director clapped his hands, a gentle applause, not without sarcasm.

"What is our current take?"

A brief silence, "One Hundred and forty-five million, we speculate that in two hours we'll have broken even just from the live broadcasts. We won't know how much we make on the betting pool until we see how it all shakes out."

The Director looked pleased with himself, "Well looks like we are off to a good start." His eyes fixed on screen #50, "What are the odds on the girl on screen fifty?"

"Victoria Smiley? She's sitting at seventeen to one."

The Director sucked in a breath, "Oh. Place a bet for me would you. Fifteen grand on her, eighteen on Teddy and sixteen on Family Man."

"Being done now."

The Director scratched his chin, gave considered look to the editor, who had stepped in for this question "Who is your money on?"

A wiry man in his early 30's, between his lips a cigarette hung. He pulled it out, blew a smoke ring. The director watched him think about the question while considering his plaid shirt and T-shirt, of course it was printed with the Polish poster for Battle Royale.

"Teddy and Moe."

"I like the look of that creature Moe, put three on him."

"Will do." The line went dead.

The Director got comfortable and began to lose himself in the screens, he could orchestrate or spectate, each required careful watching.

Chapter Six: Duck Season

Victoria slowed from a jog to a creep as she came to the edge of the woods.

Before her was a lake with a boathouse, a newish building built with big windows and a timber frame that led to a long jetty. The sky was cloudless and the entire lake was glittering under the sharp light of the morning sun. She did not want to be seen. Victoria dropped down behind a fallen tree. Her eyes surveying the forty feet between her and the boathouse, long grass swaying in the morning's wind pushed over by the wind, rising as the gusts waned before falling over again.

"Is it worth the risk?"

Her eyes caught something.

A man was walking to the building.

Her hand found the handle of her Bowie knife, slowly pulling it free.

She hopped the tree and landed crouched, a hand on the ground. She began to crawl on the tips of her fingers and toes. She closed the distance between them quickly but kept below the grass level. He entered the boathouse.

Oliver Fawkes had been a soldier before the Massacre, he'd been a devil. A man paid to kill he'd followed war where it came, gutting, shooting and taking no prisoners. Nothing had changed.

He walked across the boathouse club room towards the bar. He bent over it and found a bottle of Jack Daniels, he'd been there enough times could've been gulping it down but he dug deeper, grabbed a bottle of Bullet and a glass, it went down easy. He knew the truth, that he would win, that he had what it took to murder forty-three people, given what he'd done, the men he'd laid to waste it wasn't much. Oliver strode across the room.

He was planning to lay low till the morning then spring his assault across the island. He spun the axe in his hands, his left hand nearly still around the heel as his right rolled the bowed shaft around and around..

"I'm a fucking winner."

"No, you're not."

His hands went limp. The axe hit the floor. Another thud on the island..

Oliver's eyes went wide.

"I…I…I"

Something cold slid from his back as he dropped to his knees.

"I….I…"

Cold steel rested under his chin before numbness and warmth spread down his body.

It was already done.

He'd not even heard Victoria coming up behind him.

She stood over her victim, he still spluttered and twitched.

Victoria had cut his throat far beyond what was required, that knife had raked across bone, she felt the broken tip catch. She let out the breath she'd been holding and turned from him, walking to the bar and fetching a bottle of water. With a squeeze and a few gulps, it was gone, two more went in her pack. She did the math's on Oliver and the others, she'd now be up to one million pounds.. She sighed and left, not bothering to look at the stranger's body, she knew he was dead.

Victoria exited back into the world and onto the jetty that led into the lake.

On either side where small sail boats. All of the same design but different colours.

"Jesus," She muttered to herself, "how much money do they put into this?"

A shiver shot down her spine. She knew she was being watched.

Victoria closed her eyes, "A million is more than enough."

The wood beside her turned in to splinters as a bullet slid by her, the damage let a canoe float free. Reflex had her dive into the shimmering water. The cold shot long needles deep into her muscles almost causing her to breathe. Through the dark she felt a bullet torpedo past her in the water.

She began to kick and swim.

On the other side of the lake a slender finger released from the trigger as the sniper looked through her scope. She licked her teeth and quickly moved, slinging the rifle over her shoulder. Mary bit down on her tongue as she ran. She'd just wasted two bullets on the lucky bitch.

Victoria erupted from the surface of the water, unable to take it anymore, gasping for air. Her eyes darted around trying to get a notion where those shots could have come from. She saw no one, she might still be in their sights.

Her muscles were slowing in the cold.

Even on this summer's evening the water was brutally cold, draining everything from within her muscles were as likely to shiver and stall as they were to do what she asked them to. She crawled into the mud and slogged through it clutching her bag strap.

She had her provisions.

Victoria collapsed shivering in the sludge.

"No."

The word crept from her throat.

She knew why.

If she stopped, her sniper would get another chance. Victoria forced herself to her knees, the shivering hitting her core.

The drugs, the cold and adrenaline.

Everything was hitting her.

Slowly she forced her legs beneath her and stood.

Then she ran, just running no longer planning and considering but running all the same.

Chapter Seven: Disagreeing with a coin

The Dog stood listening.

The gun shot echoed around him.

"Why have you stopped?" snapped the cruel voice in his ear.

"Some...somebody is shooting." The Dog stuttered out.

"Then look that way, show me you useless waste of cum, don't make me guess."

Dog moved his head and the camera attached to his earpiece looked around the dark, empty wood he now found himself in.

"You are alone mutt. There isn't anyone here."

The Dog chewed his lip, "Bu…bu...but…"

"First you get lost in a bog, second you get distracted by music and now you're getting spooked by gunshots in the distance. For fucks sake you stupid fucking piece of shit, I've watched you tear through doors and crush men's bones with your bare hands. Now after all that you're getting scared? You know the rules about being scared."

"Yes…"

"And what are they?"

"I'm only allowed to be scared of you." The Dog said clearly looking down at his wet boots.

"That's fucking right. You stop again, I will punish you."

"Please…don't…"

"Then get out there and kill something!"

Dog began to run.

His hulking frame tearing through the woods with his club in hand.

Teddy strolled down the hill whistling Modern Major General.

Looking around the declining grass he could see the miles that lay before him.

Directly in front of him were woods, beyond that, a brutish structure stood. The simple outline of heavy stonework, some sort of castle.

To his left he could make out a town and what seemed to be houses.

Teddy stopped in his tracks.

He knew what was to the right, the small port he'd picked up his unwilling, somewhat rude cuisine at.

He reached up and scratched his chin under his mask.

"Has to be a romp through the woods to the castle or a straight walk to the town, decisions decisions." He said to himself.

He dug into his pocket and pulled out a shiny 50p.

He toyed with it on his thumb, "Heads for castle tails for town."

He flicked it into the air and caught it, tipping it onto the back of his other hand.

"Hmm tails." Teddy said disappointingly. He flicked the coin over his shoulder, "Broken coin doesn't know that castles are much more fun."

Teddy began to cartwheel down the hill singing Modern Major General. He seemed happy with his disagreement with the 50p coin that now lay half hidden in the grass.

Gary was now walking around the coast of the island.

His eyes drawn to the plumes of smoke drifting from the top of the hill. It unsettled him to think of what madness must have occurred up there. He was worried.

He'd not seen anyone since the devil in the mask kidnapped the man in the store. Something caught his eye in the sky above him. What seemed to be a small plane was circling above him.

"An unmanned plane most likely...maybe even a drone." He thought.

It unnerved him to know that above, someone was always watching. He gripped his Uchigatana tighter as he dropped from the ladder onto the street. The sound of crashing and echoing gunshots still hung in the air in the small town behind him, but this was not the fight he was looking for. He had a purpose here, but he'd yet to come across it.

Haru found himself wading through waist high grass with the false suburbs to his back.

He winced as nettles stung at his knees and shins through his trousers. His jacket caught and snagged on hidden brambles. The assassin found himself cursing as his anger grew. Suddenly his foot sank and was sucked down by hidden water.

He'd entered the bog. Haru found his other foot a log to stand on and pulled his other free.

Splashing echoed through the air as Haru's hand found his gun. Ahead of him the grass thinned out as he ducked into the water.

He peered through the green stalks.

In the distance a man ran towards him, Haru took aim.

"Help me!" the man screamed before a bullet tore through his chest.

Haru ducked down as the man fell and skidded to a stop in the murky water. From behind him Haru watched as a group of five gathered around the thrashing man. He lowered his gun.

Leading them was a reasonably handsome man in his fifties wearing glasses.

He looked down at the wounded man, "You should have just said yes to me."

With that he turned away only for a thin weasel like man in a short sleeved pink bowling shirt to step forward and shoot the wounded man in the back of the head. Haru held his breath as the group stripped the dead man of what he'd been carrying and disappeared off into the bog. After a moment too long, he allowed himself to breath once more and began to back out of the bog.

Chapter Eight: Wonder if she's single?

Victoria collapsed against the giant stone wall that rose up to meet her.

Her lungs burned from her chaotic run through the forest away from the lake. Controlling herself, she stopped the panicked breaths and took slow measured ones, until she felt her heart slow to a controlled beat and that the burning receded to somewhere deep down as a dull ache.

She looked up at the towering stone wall before her. Ancient dark stones made up the castle that she now found herself against, old, weathered, substantial and weighted with time. Her cold hand felt for her gun and pulled it free.

Slowly she crept around the wall until the huge archway opened before her; the large ancient wooden gate lay open. She brought her Rossi up and slowly stepped inside.

Victoria stepped into a vast courtyard that housed mannequins in medieval attire.

Peasants, knights, blacksmiths, jesters.

She realized they were the same dead eyed make as those who were in the shopping center.

Victoria slowly walked in close to one of the blacksmiths, around the mannequin was a number of weapons.

Swords, mace's, axes, spears, knives all of which looked to be in fully working order.

A screech of metal on metal dragged behind her. Victoria spun and with no hesitation pulled the trigger only to hear the clang of the ricocheting bullet.

She caught a blur as her target dove behind a cart.

Victoria knelt behind the blacksmith beside her as a muzzle poked from over the cart and shots cracked out in her general direction.

The blacksmith's arm exploded as Victoria gritted her teeth and crept around his anvil.

Teddy heard the echoes of shots and skidded to a halt outside of the great archway.

"Oh! There's a show!" He cried giddily before running right past the archway and scaling the wall itself like some deranged howler monkey.

Victoria sprung holding the Rossi in both hands and fired at the figure behind the cart, only once again to hear the ricochet of bullets.

The figure slowly stood, head to toe in black armoured riot gear.

"Bugger."

The rioter raised their gun, an antique looking luger, and fired. Victoria was already diving up the steps and through the door above as bullets cracked on the stone around her.

Teddy found a heavily barred window, he hung from them and looked through as his feet gripped the sloped sill..

He looked into a large banquet hall.

Across the large space there were long tables covered in food, though much to his annoyance, the spectacularly portioned feast appeared to be plastic. His eyes slid around to her as she slid into the room closing the door behind herself.

Lanterns along the walls sparked into life illuminating the space, Teddy could see her properly now, his attention was undivided.

"Oooo here we go." Teddy giggled to himself.

Victoria braced herself against the door.

She could hear footfalls beyond closing in on the door. The impact threw her to the floor as the door buckled under a crushing blow. She grabbed her arm as pain shot through it. A long sliver of wood stuck out of it horribly. Most of the door held but she could hear the rioter running away, preparing for another run up. She forced herself to stand.

Teddy watched as the woman ran across the room, throwing things from the tables before stopping and sprinting to one of the lanterns on the wall.

This had piqued his curiosity. The door thumped again harder and Teddy could see its hinges where close to failing.

"This is getting exciting."

If he hadn't been holding on to the bars he'd have been clapping.

Victoria had seconds to finish. Her hands hurt from the hot metal as she fumbled the DIY contraption together, just in time to hear the door give way and the rioter to come crashing into the room.

She raised the device and pulled the makeshift trigger.

Teddy actually found himself gasping in excitement as the woman turned to face her foe brandishing one of the lanterns from the wall still attached by a long hose.

The reason he was so excited was that she'd broken the safety valve away, and instead of giving off an inch of flame, it was now several feet of unbridled fiery fury.

Victoria fired out long bursts of flame at the rioter who had no time to hide.

The suit caught on fire as the rioter flailed desperately trying to douse the flames. She kept up on the screaming figure as they fell over the table. The rioter crumpled; their last strangled breaths inaudible over the roar of the growing flames.

Teddy watched as the figure was lost in flames and the fire was spreading. He watched her surrounded by the flames like a gory goddess.

"Beautiful…perfectly beautiful...I wonder if she's single?"

Teddy smiled under his mask and let go, falling to the ground below with surprising agility.

"I'll just have to kill her later…maybe over a nice candlelit dinner...or a movie."

Victoria dropped her flame thrower as the flames spread everywhere. The rioter was lost in the carnage. She leapt towards the door as the heat filled her lungs. Her escape left nothing but carnage.

The castle had stood for over five hundred years and it was now burning. The fire spread to the gas mains which tore through to the tanks. The explosion shattered the foundation of the castle and it fell in upon itself becoming a smouldering dolmen for the now silent rioter.

Chapter Nine: Good Dog

The Dog stood quietly looking up into the sky.

Over the tree line he could see a rising tower of smoke.

"Looks like you've found someone." Growled his handler, "Sick 'em."

The monstrous figure exploded into a sprint, tearing through the woods towards the smoke. His slow mind filled with commands, bite them, break them, kill them. All the words that his owner would say to him before he'd have to hurt someone.

He erupted from the woods into the clearing. His eyes widened. Before him the castle was an inferno. Yellow flames licked up the old stone walls while black smoke fumed from the top. A grey choking mist now rose around the castle.

The Dog swallowed trying to hold back the tears as it stung his eyes.

"Keep looking!" the owner screeched.

The Dog looked around in a panic.

He caught sight of someone running, a small figure just disappearing over the top of the small hill that led up from the castle. He took off running.

Over the small hill beside the castle a small town rose up to meet him. He began to run toward it howling madly.

If he found someone it would make his owner happy.

If he killed them, he'd be called a good boy.

He'd not have to be afraid.

His feet found asphalt as he stumbled onto a road that abruptly ended just outside of the town.

His legs began to burn as he stormed down the main street.

"Slow down you fucking idiot!" His owner angrily commanded, "The fucker might have a gun."

"I don… don… don't like guns." The Dog stuttered out of fear.

"Slow down and be quiet, go inside one of the shops and we'll start there."

Victoria watched in horror as the behemoth lumbered into the pharmacy below her hiding spot. Quickly she tied off the bandage around her arm where she'd pried the long splinter of wood from. She began to pack away her supplies when the door to her room opened.

The Dog entered the office above the pharmacy.

It was small. He felt like the walls were too small for him. He hated being so big.

In the office was a desk, computer, files, a swivel chair behind the desk, a small chair before the desk and a sofa against the wall.

Something on the sofa caught his eye. He leaned over and looked at it.

A bag much like the one that didn't fit around his shoulders had a holster with a gun in it, bloodied bandages and a pair of tweezers with a long sliver of wood in it.

Victoria held her breath under the desk, holding her bowie knife and jacket.

She wished she'd not taken off her gun belt.

"Someone's here." Said her giant hunter with a voice that surprised her, it was quiet, soft spoken and almost childlike. What followed was a low buzz of someone speaking through an earpiece.

She could feel her heart pumping, how could

he not hear it? All she had was the knife and he was huge. She looked up at the underside of the table, praying he'd leave.

The Dog stood slowly, eyeing up the room.

"Is there someone here?"

A creak echoed out from under his footsteps, he sniffed the air smelling the faint odour of smoke.

"I know you're here."

He looked down at the small desk.

"Are you hiding?"

The Dog had begun to step around it when someone launched out from under the table and startled him.

The tiny woman snatched at the keyboard from the table and before he could do anything smashed it across his face. Pained, he screamed as he struck out blindly, catching her, and threw her.

Victoria felt the glass as she ploughed through it, feeling the open air welcome her, to the fall and the unforgiving embrace of the tarmac below.

The Dog screamed and held his face.

He was waiting for it.

The screaming.

The names.

The insults.

But they didn't come.

The Dog felt to his earpiece and pulled it free.
It was broken.

The Dog collapsed to his knees with the small
broken device held within his enormous hands.
He was alone. He didn't know what to do.

The giant began to cry.

Chapter Ten: The black deep

The world was now pain.

Victoria moved slowly, trying to stop herself from going into shock.

Every nerve ending screamed back in response. She pushed herself to her knees, watching as blood fell to the pavement from her now broken nose.

She had to stand. Slowly she raised herself to her feet. She had to run.

Forcibly she began to put one foot in front of the other, as her entire left side echoed with the mind dulling blades of pain. As she moved slowly, building up from a stumble to a limp, she pushed her right arm into the jacket and pulled it over her left shoulder.

From afar Mary could see the pillar of smoke rising into the sky above. She sprinted towards the carnage.

Victoria felt the creeping numbness from her left hand. She didn't want to look down. She didn't want to acknowledge that she'd been hurt.

Victoria came to a railing and stopped, falling

against it. Her mind raced thinking the worst. Bones broken. Fractured skull. Internal bleeding.

She peered over the railing.

Water, it was moving fast.

A small river seemed to run through this town and as she looked over, she could see it ran out to sea.

Victoria began to pull herself along the railing. Before her as the railing tailed off onto a bridge, it led to the other half of the town.

She stumbled onto it.

Mary strode into town, her rifle slung across her back with a pistol in her hand. The town was quiet.

The Dog looked out the window and saw the witch. He hid under the desk with his feet poking out. He couldn't stop the tears.

He was terrified.

Mary looked at the broken glass and the trail of blood. "Hello there." She holstered her pistol and pulled her rifle into position.

Victoria could now see black spots dance across her vision with every pain inducing step she took.

She wanted to be sick.

She wanted to cry.

She wanted to scream out with the agony that was brewing inside of her body.

She wanted to die.

Mary looked through the scope of the rifle and smiled. In her sights she could see the woman who'd gotten lucky. She took aim.

Victoria stopped in her tracks. She'd made enough money. She knew this.

Penelope didn't need any more.

The trigger squeezed.

The shot fired.

The bullet travelled through the space between muzzle and target.

The spinning piece of lead punched through the wind, knocking it off course by a mere half inch.

Victoria had blacked out before the bullet hit.

"Yes!" Mary hissed through clenched teeth as her target spun wildly and fell over the railing of the bridge. She watched as the limp figure splashed into the running torrent flowing beneath the bridge. "Jesus, that was satisfying."

She hung her rifle back up and trotted away, ecstatic she'd made half a million.

Under her breath she murmured "Not so lucky now, bitch."

Chapter Eleven: Here there be Monsters

Two men crossed the fake runway, the dead shells of planes stood in rows either side of the long stretch of tarmac. One being a young Hungarian man in his twenties armed with an assault rifle, the other being a broad-shouldered Swedish man armed with a stubby machine gun. It had barely passed four o'clock in the afternoon and they'd made two and a half million between them.

They were experienced soldiers yet neither saw it.

Silently climbing up and over the wing of one of the dead planes crawled a horrible creature. A thin layer of skin over lean muscle and sinew. Long thin limbs. Bone China skin. Not a single hair on his body. All framing those soulless blood red eyes.

Moe.

He effortlessly and silently fell from the wing, landing onto the balls of his feet.

He only wore grey and black camouflaged combat trousers and what seemed to be grey gutties on his feet.

A small pack was all that he carried across the small of his back. With other-worldly calmness, he reached into his pack and drew two long thin silver knifes, held between the two fingers of his right hand. His crimson eyes judged the short distance between his prey and their demise.

In one almost balletic motion he spun, sending the two knifes flying. Both thwacked into the base of each of their skulls causing them to fall dead instantly.

Moe walked lightly over to the two, plucking the throwing knifes from the corpses. Ignoring the guns, he began to loot their rucksacks for food and water.

Pinball Wizard played from an ancient 8 track. A twitching sadist picked up the hammer. The neo-Nazi with the Oedipus complex surveyed it with his manic, wide, shaking eyes. Bringing it to his mouth he bit the claw of it happily.

Marlow

His bloodied captive strained against the binds of the chair and cried into his gag. Marlow gently tapped the hammer off of the man's forehead. His captive screamed into the gag trying to pull away. Marlow scratched the small swastika tattoo in the middle of his forehead.

"You are one sexy fucker you know that." Marlow said while licking his lips, "Now I'm not going to fuck you…though the thought has crossed my mind. No, I've not got time for that." He caressed the man's cheek with the claw of the hammer, "No but I do feel I should earn that half million for killing you."

His captive's eyes were wide, willing the man to drop dead.

"So, to begin with I'm going to remedy something that's been annoying me."

Marlow swung the hammer with a bone crunching blow into the man's jaw, leaving him blinking in and out of consciousness, blood and teeth fragments pouring down his throat and from his mouth.

The crooked toothed sadist smiled, "You've got too many fucking teeth."

Bora stood with his heavy Kukri blade in hand while the woman loaded her pistol.

She lifted the gun and pulled the trigger. The Brazilian moved with impossible speed and sliced the bullet out of the air. She stared back in complete horror as he began to approach her with his curved blade pointed at her. She panicked and brought the gun to her temple pulling the trigger.

Her body slumped to the ground as Bora knelt by it, "Such a disappointment."

Family Man stood looking at the charred wood, flesh and bones, he didn't have much beyond slight furrow in his brow over the scene.

He sucked his teeth, "You see this fella, it takes a true psychopath to do this to a man."

Jesus approached him, a weasel like man in a gaudy pink shirt, "Teddy is a true psychopath Sir."

"That is true." muttered Family Man.

His group were scavenging what they could from the tower of speakers Teddy had left beside his BBQ.

"Remember boys, if you see that mask wearing freak I don't want you going up against him alone, you'll end up like this poor bastard who's insides are all over this hill..." he stared at the recliner, "...or have your head left in such an undignified fashion."

Family Man picked it up and dropped it into the empty pyre beside the rest of him.

"I hope that degenerate finished you quick son. I really do." Family Man said while wiping his hands on his jeans, the stains left on them seemed to give him more pause than the horrors they had all just inspected.

Chapter Twelve: Rising storm

Gary walked along the coast listening to the waves crash below him.

The dark grey clouds approaching from the horizon were making the sea angry. The clown could feel the heat leaving the air as the storm approached. He could see the rain fall beneath the cloud.

Tonight, was going to be a rough one. Gary pulled his coat closer as the wind began to blow harder from the sea. As he turned to walk on, something caught his eye.

A body in the water.

Victoria had been dreaming in the water.

Swaying thoughts and crashing images.

The birthday cake with the four candles.

The sad little girl staring back at her.

It was a nightmare of melancholy and regret.

Victoria screamed herself awake.

Lurching out of the dream she vaulted up right, pain exploding through her body. She collapsed gasping in the new agony she'd given herself.

"Good Evening."

She turned her head to see the man sitting across from her, a clown with deeply smeared make up.

She cleared her dry throat, "Your mascara is running."

"That's what happens when you jump into the Irish Sea to rescue someone."

"Why?"

"I'm a nice person."

"You're playing the massacre…you're not a nice person."

The clown stretched his legs out, "I used to not be a nice person if that helps. Are you a nice person?"

Victoria closed her eyes and rested her head back onto what thankfully seemed to be a pillow, "I'm not even sure I can be counted as a person anymore."

"How do you mean?"

"I don't care about anyone."

"Sociopath?" The clown asked.

Victoria grimaced while trying to move,

feeling something hold her right arm in place, "Is this therapy now?"

"I'm sure all of us on this island could use it.", mused the clown, "Before you try, your uninjured hand is handcuffed to the table."

Victoria could feel it now, the cold ring of metal around her wrist.

She raised her other hand slowly, a thick bandage held both her little and its neighbouring finger together.

"You've a broken finger, a few bruised ribs, though one may be cracked but can't tell, and one giant bruise on your back."

Victoria smiled, "My jacket…"

The clown pointed to a corner of the warm rustic room she was now starting to notice, "It's over there with a knife. You didn't have anything else when I found you."

"I left them…well I had to, someone threw me out a window."

"Ouch anyone I'd know?"

Victoria shook her head, "I don't know anyone's names."

"Oh. Hi, I'm Gary the clown."

Victoria looked him over, "Hello Gary the clown I'm Victoria."

"Hello Victoria. So, tell me how you ended up in the sea?"

"You tell me why you didn't let me drown."

Gary smiled through his smeared make up, "You answer mine and I'll answer yours."

"Someone shot me."

"I didn't find any holes."

Victoria squirmed trying to find a position that didn't cause her muscles to ache, "Check my jacket."

Gary stood and walked across the room picking the jacket off of a small coffee table. Victoria's mind was beginning to wake up properly now, she could see she was in a living room/kitchen and that she was lying on an old wooden table. A fire roared in an old stone fireplace while metal stairs circled up to a floor above.

Gary held the coat finger, a small piece of material that was torn.

"Is this body armour?"

"Fancy Kevlar weave."

Gary laughed, "You snuck body armour in, you are certainly a crafty one."

Victoria laughed shallowly, "If it had been a straight shot it would have gone right through, I think the shooter just winged me."

"Lucky you." Smiled Gary as he lay back into his chair.

Victoria looked at him and he held her gaze, "Why did you save me?"

"Well I'm not here to kill people. I'm here to kill only one person. One single person and then I'm done."

"If you leave they'll…"

"I don't plan on leaving." He said solemnly, "These are my last days on this world and once I kill him I'll be satisfied to move on."

"Who?"

"You don't know any names so why does it matter?"

"It matters to you and I'm not going anywhere."

"His name is Bora."

"Bora?"

"Yep, so why are you here?"

"I thought we were still on Bora."

"Revenge is a spectacularly boring thing to talk about. It's grim and serious and I dislike the subject. Still fairly disappointed in myself that it's become a fixation for me. So, if you don't mind me asking why are you here?"

"For the money." Victoria grimaced.

"Well if you win it's a lot of money."

"I don't need to win. I just need the money."

"For someone else?" Gary asked calmly.

Victoria pointed with her bandaged hand, "Right pocket, there is something sewn into it."

Gary looked down at the jacket that he still held, he reached inside of the pocket and felt. Something small and hard pressed against his fingertips.

"Tear it out."

Gary held the pocket lining and pulled the material free. A small thin metal capsule fell out.

"Open it."

Slowly he unscrewed it and inside was

something rolled up. He pulled it out and unrolled it. Before him was a small passport sized photo of a happy child.

"She yours?"

"Yes."

"And the money goes to her?"

"Yes."

"I thought you didn't care about anyone."

Victoria's eyes watered as something held back almost made it to the surface, "She's not just anyone."

Gary gently rolled the photo up and put it back into the metal capsule, "She'll miss her mother."

"She has one…I gave her up for adoption when she was four." Victoria stared off into space, "I am not fit to be…"

Gary held up his hand, "You made your choice. She seems a happy, lovely little girl. Does she have a name?"

"Penelope."

"Lovely name."

"It's the only thing I've ever given her."

"Well you gave her life plus whatever you've made over the last 24 hours."

"Million and a half."

Gary let out a whistle, "Impressive. What story have you set up?"

"Inheritance from her birth mother to be put into an account she can't access till she's 18."

"That's lovely. Well aside from the blood money of course. Mine goes to my brother and his family."

"No family of your own?"

"Why do you think I want to kill Bora." Gary said calmly.

"Sorry."

The sound of thunder rolled around them as rain began to hit the outside of the building.

Victoria looked about, "Where are we?"

"We are in a cottage that is at the base of a lighthouse."

"It's not on right now is it?"

"No, I disabled it as soon as I got you settled."

"Good…what guns have you?"

"None."

"None?" Asked the confused Victoria.

"I only carry what I arrived with." He gestured to his swords leaning against the wall.

"Katanas?"

"No but they are Japanese."

"How'd you get them?"

Gary smiled, "My late wife was Japanese and her father was one of the few practicing Samurai left...well she called him a weekend Samurai."

"Really?"

"Yep. Very traditional. Followed Bushido to the letter. Was a master with those blades."

"He gave them to you?"

"Well after Bora…. after what happened he trained me to use them. Taught me everything."

"So, you're a Samurai?"

"Kind of."

"And the clown stuff?"

"My daughter liked clowns." He said with a

smile at the memory.

Thunder shook the room again.

Gary stared up at the ceiling, "Summer storm, must be right over us now." He stood stretching. "Are you hungry? I found some food… I say food more of some vegetable soup mix. Should be ready by now."

"You'll have to uncuff me."

Gary looked at the cuff, "I will wont I."

Victoria ate the soup slowly, the first proper food she'd eaten over the entire massacre. Gary ate facing her with one hand using the spoon and the other wrapped around the handle of his long Uchigatana blade that rested on his lap.

He smiled to himself, "I know I made this myself and it would be egotistical to like such a thing but damn…this is tasty soup."

"It's nice."

He swallowed another mouthful. "I really wish I had some white crusty bread."

"With some butter." Victoria smiled then stopped, "How am I making myself hungrier while eating?"

"Could be worse…we could be talking about

steak.”

“Or roast chicken.”

“Or a bowl of stew.”

“Or pasta.”

Gary shook his head, “It’s maddening to think like this about food. This,” He pointed to the bowls in front of them with his spoon, “is probably the last meal we’ll ever have.”

Victoria shrugged, “At least the company is good.”

“Well I am amazing.” Smiled the clown.

“Fuck!” She said abruptly, “I want a fucking cup of coffee so badly.”

“I’d settle for some wine.”

They both laughed enjoying their meals.

Chapter Thirteen: Complaining to management

Teddy ran into the open door, water dripping off of him as the night time storm raged behind him.

"I should have brought an umbrella." Muttered the unhappy masked psychopath kicking water from his well-tailored, though rather soggy trousers.

He looked around his new environment.

It was the main hallway of a school. He began to walk down the corridor his shoes squishing and squeaking.

"Ah looks just like the one I remember…more screaming kids then though." He poked his head into a classroom, "Teddy don't pull the girls hair." He flicked through books scattered on the tables, "Teddy don't throw snails at the headmaster." He stood at the blackboard and picked up the chalk, "Teddy don't set Mr. Philips on fire."

Teddy spun away leaving 'Teddy was here' scrawled across the blackboard. Back into the corridor he stopped and felt around his neck.

"I dropped my ears."

He looked down to the front door, the water truly pouring now.

He shrugged, "Eh I'll just get some more."

A crash echoed up above him.

"Hmmm some others must be here for after school clubs. I hope it's the gaming group, I'm totally up for a bit of late-night D&D."

Teddy skipped up the stairs taking them three at a time before stopping abruptly at the top, "Silly Ducky no running in the corridors."

He walked (albeit it briskly) towards the sound of crashing. He stopped by an open door and peered in, just in time to see a man in a red football t-shirt drop a school table onto the back of a giant man.

To Teddy's surprise the giant man seemed to be weeping. The football hooligan tossed another chair at the weeping colossus, "Fucking do something you retard!"

Teddy stepped in as the chair left the hooligan's hand and stopped behind him.

"Enough of this now."

And in one moment, he reached forward

grabbing his head and snapped the man's neck.

The corpse slumped to the floor.

Teddy stepped over him and cautiously approached the shaking form in the middle of the floor.

"Now this is a tad out of character for me, but I have to ask this, are you ok?"

The big man looked up, his face beaten and cut, his eyes red and swollen.

"You're a teddy bear."

"It's a life choice."

The huge man threw his arms around Teddy's waist and hugged him tightly, "Thank yo…yo…you for making the ba…bad man stop."

Teddy stood bolt upright his hands up and uncomfortably fidgeted, "I won't lie…I've no idea how to feel about the whole hugging thing."

The large man let go and stood up in turn completely dwarfing Teddy by the better part of a foot, "I'm S..s…sorry I…"

Teddy threw his hands up, "Oh its fine just wasn't expecting it." He looked at his latest victim the hooligan, "Now you seem to be a man of…stature. Why didn't you just kill him."

"Owner didn't tell me too."

"Owner?"

The large man produced a small earpiece and a camera and handed it to Teddy, "Could you fix it?"

Teddy looked down at the broken earpiece and back at the man, "Could you excuse me for just one moment?"

The large man nodded slowly as Teddy backed out of the room closing the door behind him.

He took a deep breath before turning to the tiny hidden camera just above the door, "You know who I am. I demand to speak to the management. Now I passed an office downstairs with a telephone. Now I'm guessing you've got access to all of the electronics so when I get downstairs with him, I want to find it ringing and someone on the other end to explain this to me. Understand?"

Teddy opened the door only to see the large man leaning forward inches from his mask, "Who you talking t..t…to?"

"Organising a phone call, come with me will

you?"

Teddy spun on his heel and his colossal friend followed. Just as Teddy's foot touched the ground floor a phone rang.

Teddy turned to his lumbering friend, "Feel free to sit in there and wait. There are some books."

The large man smiled and wandered into the classroom as Teddy marched to the office.

He snatched up the phone and placed it to his mask.

"Good Evening Teddy."

"Oh hello I recognise that voice. You're the man from the orientation video yes? You know the one with the hair and those simply dazzling teeth."

"Yes I am and might I just say I am a huge fan of your work."

"Oh it's always nice to meet a fan," Teddy gushed happily but quickly his mood soured, "Now to this man I've just found."

"Ah Dog."

"His name is Dog?"

The Director sighed into the phone on the other end, "Yes."

"Now I don't want to seem rude, especially to him, but he doesn't seem to have complete mental faculties."

"How do you mean?"

"He is a seven-foot tall giant who seems to have the mind of a child. I'm going to assume he has some sort of problem in that area."

"From what I'm to understand it was a result of brain damage as a child."

"And why was he allowed to take part in the massacre."

"I don't follow."

Teddy's mood grew angry, "He called someone his owner, someone who makes decisions for him. He shouldn't have been admitted and you know it."

"Well," the Director began, "his brother suggested a system that would allow him to be guided and helped."

"His owner is his brother?" Teddy's hand gripped the edge of the table so tightly his knuckles whitened.

"Yes."

"Let me guess, he's also acting next of kin then."

"Yes."

"So, his brother sold him off to you."

A silence on the other end of the line.

"Teddy I never thought you to be the sensitive type."

"Oh I'd flay every single able bodied person on this island alive while singing the entire set list of Les Misérables and you know that, but this man should not be here. I want to buy him out."

"Pardon?"

"I want to buy him out; I understand that in the rules a second party other than the first party can buy the release of the first party from the Massacre."

"That is in the rules, but you can't be playing and be that party too."

"Then I invoke the rule to saying any returning champion can buy themselves out. Then I'm buying him out."

The Director's voice quivered, "But that takes your money earned away and dropped into the winning pot that you cannot enter."

Teddy stamped his foot and truly growled, "Do you think I do this for money! No this is my damned holiday away from the boring normalness of everything else. So, accept my buying me and…Dog out."

"Teddy I'm not sure I can allow…"

"I assume you're watching." Teddy said as he looked up at the nearest camera.

"I am."

"Good." Teddy proceeded to pull his pistol from his hip and place the barrel under his chin, "If you don't agree to my terms, I'll shoot myself in the head."

"Wait what?"

"I'll shoot myself in the head…I think that's pretty clear from the whole act of aiming this loaded gun at my own head…did I do it too fast for you to follow? Should I start again?"

"No, I mean what do you wish to accomplish with this?"

"Well as you've pointed out you're a fan, so you'll be heart broken. Also, I know that I'm pretty much the Massacre's unofficial mascot and bring in a ton of returning viewers who bring oh so much money along with them, so if I blow my brains out you lose viewers. Losing viewers means losing money. Losing money means the higher ups lose you. Losing you probably means some sort of horrible fate like death or making a new résumé for a job in HR, a fast food chain if you're lucky.. Am I making my point clear?"

"Fine!" the Director said through obviously gritted teeth. "That's five million for you and one and a half for him."

"That's fine."

"It will take time to organise transport for you off of the island. When such is organised you will be notified."

"Thank you," Teddy said cheerfully, "and to make sure there's no hard feelings I'll make sure to give you my autograph when I see you."

The line went dead. Teddy dropped the phone onto the receiver.

He trotted over to the classroom and poked his head into the door. Dog was sitting colouring in a picture in one of the children's books.

"Uh…Dog?"

The large man looked up smiling, "Hello Mr Teddy."

"Firstly, it's just Teddy second we'll be leaving soon."

"Leaving?"

"Yep I'm getting you away from the bad people."

The large man stood with a look of pure glee on his face, "Thank you Mr Teddy."

With one huge stride Dog picked Teddy up and gave him a giant hug.

"You know…I've decided I don't like the hugging."

Chapter Fourteen: Moment of clarity

Haru had given up.

After the bog his trousers had been ruined, his shoes were lost and now while walking through the storm he was soaked to his core.

He'd still not seen anyone since his encounter with Family Man's group.

Hours before a tower of smoke had appeared drawing him out of the bog.

By the time he'd reached the castle it was nothing more than smouldering rubble. After that he'd decided to go south along the coast.

That is when the storm hit.

Rain.

Wind.

The fury of the elements.

Haru didn't care.

He was failing his elder brother.

Solemnly he pressed on feeling the wet grass under his feet as his face was pelted with rain and wind. No kills meant no money. He could see his elder brother's face, twisted in disappointment.

"You represent us. Do not shame us."

Those were the last words he'd spoken to Haru before they'd taken him away. Everything else was a disgrace muddled blur but those words burned true.

Shame.

That is what he'd be remembered for by the Yakuza, his only family. They'd taken him in young when no one else would. A half Japanese half Korean orphan. It'd been a night like this with a storm just as angry that his elder brother found him, walking the streets as a child in rags and with no shoes.

Haru closed his eyes.

That night at the tender age of eight he believed that he was going to die in the cold and in the rain. The same belief was here only now he knew it was true.

His foot sank and he opened his eyes.

A long beach stretched out before him into the darkness, waves crashed down onto the shore violently, but silent compared to the anarchy of the storm above. Lightning lit up the sky arching down into the sea beyond.

Haru did not want to die with shame.

He strode out onto the sand and stood alone.

The money he had did not make him the man he was, so he tore his jacket and shirt from his body and stood bare chested against the storm.

He screamed.

Anger, frustration, shame all poured out of him as the storm beat against him, but he did not yield.

He let everything out and only once he had, calmness took him.

His voice rang silent and the rain stopped.

He could hear the ocean lapping against the shore.

He could see the beach and sea clearly as the cloud parted and the moon shone.

Haru breathed slowly letting everything settle in to its rightful place and for one brief moment he felt it.

Utter serenity.

He let it take him as he sat cross legged on the beach and watched the ocean. The dark waves rocked and swelled in the distance only to roll onto the shores, white for the briefest moments. He began to breathe in tandem with the sea.

The words found him.

"Be calm. Be Patient."

He stood and walked into the ocean. Once up to his waist he began to bathe in the sea.

Haru had found his calm.

The director watched Haru on his screen.

He did not share his calm. He'd been forced to take Teddy out of the Massacre. For the last hour and a half, he'd had the Executive Producers scream at him over a video call. Somehow it had been his fault that Teddy found a thread of conscience to follow. His saving grace had been that Teddy was still on camera. Bets could still be made on and against him.

This had saved his neck from the chopping block for the meantime but he knew if he let Teddy off of the island, that stay of execution would soon be revoked, fast food work would be luck in that case.

He rubbed his tired eyes and looked over the screens before him.

The clown and the lucky girl in the light house.

Bora stalking someone.

Mary sleeping in the trunk of a car.

His eyes found the feed from the cabin. The last night he'd seen only Victoria resting in the bathtub. Now the cabin was full.

Six men and two women where there.

Family Man's group.

The Director knew Family Man's background and he wondered.

He smiled, standing out of his chair.

He laughed to himself happily as he made his way to bed.

The Director had found his calm, but that wouldn't be quite as idyllic as the beach.

Chapter Fifteen: Breakfast

Victoria awoke with a start; she could not remember falling asleep.

She looked around the room. She was entirely alone.

Victoria stood slowly.

There was a note written on the table.

"Thank you for last night.

It was nice to have a conversation with someone decent before the end, but I feel that I should be gone by the time you wake up, thought it would be easier this way. I've left some soup in the pot for breakfast.

Gary.

PS I sewed up your jacket putting the photo back where it belongs. She has your eyes."

Victoria stood silently in the noiseless room. She'd not been prepared for this kindness. She walked towards the jacket picking it up and with great effort she slipped it on with pain rippling through her back with each movement, all the simple motions now distinct, individual and painful in their own ways. Her eyes rolled into the back of her eyes and she breathed slowly.

She was not near the end of this, it was only the third day of the Massacre.

She clipped her Bowie knife to her belt and felt inside of her pocket, feeling for the hidden photograph.

Victoria cursed herself looking at the broken wrist watch, reminding her of everything she'd gathered and lost.

Her gun.

Water.

Food.

Food, she looked to the kitchen counter, a small pot and a bowl beside. Upon seeing it her stomach growled and twisted. She clicked the gas on and prepared her second helping of soup.

Teddy strode through the faux suburban home with mannequins staring at him.

Behind his mask he sucked his teeth, "The eyes always creeped me out."

"M…m…me too." His colossal companion said, sitting on a sofa and making it look like an armchair.

Teddy flicked the daddy mannequin between the eyes and it fell backwards landing on and crushing one of its children.

Dog jumped.

Teddy observed this, "Now it surprises me you're so jumpy."

"I scare easily."

"Why? A big, strong guy like you? You should be the one doing the scaring."

"Owner said…"

"The owner can… and please excuse my French, but he can kiss my fuzzy backside." Teddy said while stamping a foot, absentmindedly crushing daddy mannequin's knee.

Dog giggled nervously at the notion.

His head snapped around to the back of the house, "Do you think this fake house has any real food?"

Dog looked up with a smile.

"You're hungry too." Teddy fished into his pocket and picked out a candy bar. "You have this while I see if there's any bacon."

Dog took it looking at it in his hand, "Owner says dogs can't have chocolate."

Teddy made fists, whitening his knuckles, but his voice left his mask calmly, kindly even, "It's my gift to you and when we're out of here I'm going to have a few choice words with your 'owner'…possibly with a buzz saw or a mallet. Eat the chocolate, you'll like it."

Dog smiled, opened the bar and ate the chocolate down in one bite.

Haru had been walking for hours but showed no sign of tiring.

He had left most of his clothes on the beach and now walked bare foot in only his trousers, with his bag hung over his back and his pistol on his hip.

He'd headed east along the coast, past the still smoking ruins of the castle, and found the town with the bridge.

A shot rang out close by.

Pistol drawn he stepped through the streets. He could hear people arguing.

"Why did you fucking shoot her!"

"Because you wanted to fuck her!"

Haru peered around the corner to see a small playground.

Two men stood above the body of a woman missing a large chunk of the back of her head.

"She was going to die anyway why not give her a goodbye ride." Smiled one of them.

"You are one sick fuck you know that." Said the other, disgusted, but he didn't move to kill the other.

Haru slowly took aim at the smiling man and pulled the trigger. In a crack and a puff the man's cheek and ear exploded into a pink mist, causing the other to dive for cover.

Screaming echoed through the playground as automatic fire impacted the wall Haru knelt behind.

He closed his eyes and counted, still hearing the screaming over the gun fire. The thunder cracked on until the silence came with a click.

Haru stepped around the corner with gun raised and plugged him between the eyes. The man's body collapsed onto the screaming man who tried to kick and crawl away.

Haru fired into his face while a look of cold calculation took over his face.

Slowly the killer breathed and slowed his thumping heart.

This is why he was here, he'd made his first million.

Chapter Sixteen: Family first

Jesus sat on the high-backed chair in the living room of the cabin, his leg bouncing.

"I am the way, the truth and the light." He muttered.

"Pardon?"

Jesus looked up to see Family Man standing in the doorway.

"Nothing," Jesus lied, "just talking to myself."

"Ok, I've something to show you." He gestured for Jesus to follow him.

He led Jesus past the others who'd joined them over the days and into the bedroom. Jesus squirmed as Family Man approached the bed sitting down.

"Come here Chris."

Jesus approached and stood before the bed. Family Man reached under the pillow and produced what seemed to be a cellular phone.

Jesus looked confused, "Did you smuggle it in?"

"Nope found it this morning, it was strapped

beneath the bed. I think they've a few of these hidden about the island just in case the organisers need to contact players."

"Isn't that against the rules?"

"Well in this game there aren't many rules but yes this is against the rules…I got called."

Jesus swallowed dryly, "Who called?"

"I think it was the man who was in that video we all seen at wake up, but he has a mission for us."

"A mission?"

"He wants us to kill Teddy."

Jesus sat down on the bed beside him, "I know we are going after him eventually, but we're not ready."

Family man patted his knee, "You know my plan. We kill everyone on this island then we kill each other in a fair match. Now our little caller seems to like our little endeavour, so he called to give us support on the condition we kill him."

"Support."

"He's given me coordinates to a stash of weapons to the west, in that town half of this lot woke up, now I can't march them back there with no reason, I need you to suggest we go there in front of the others. Make it seem like it was your idea."

 "How?"

 "Well he told me you woke up in a room near there, do you think you can think of something that's there we can say we need?"

 "There was a bus there. It had an engine unlike all the husks."

 "See that's a good thing."

 "Then we get the weapons and kill Teddy?"

 "You catch on fast Chris."

 Jesus's brow furrowed, "But why does he want us to kill Teddy in particular?

 Family man sucked his teeth for a second, "He did not say, but damn did he sound mighty pissed at the little psycho but listen up, if you win you can ask him yourself."

 Jesus smiled, at no point had Family Man ever given the impression that any of them wouldn't win. To him everyone in his group was an equal and thus deserved a proper crack at winning the prize, the endgame seemed like it would tomorrow's problem forever when he spoke of it.

  Victoria trekked across open country with a small knapsack she'd found in the light house. Her only supplies were two plastic bottles of water, thermos of soup and her knife.

  Victoria was heading north towards red struts of scaffolding she could see in the distance. With her curiosity piqued, Victoria made for it, all the while her hand held onto the handle of her knife.

  As she got closer, she could see it now.

  The scaffolding was jutting out of a large dug up area that looked to be an archaeology dig. Half forming out of the soil and stone of the earth were walls and roads.

  "A buried town?" She said to herself as she walked around it.

  It occurred to her that the castle may not be the only sign of medieval life on the island.

  Atop of the ancient masonry of the buildings, makeshift roofs where attached, made of plywood and metal sheeting.

  The thought spiked through her head, "What are they protecting in there?"

She began to climb down the scaffolding, her shoulder screaming, reminding her that she was still injured. She dropped with a splash landing, waist deep in mud and sludge, a by-product of the previous night's storm.

"Shit." She groaned as she pulled her boots free, before making the slog toward the stone walled house closest to her.

Victoria dragged herself through the open door and peered inside.

A mannequin stared back at her.

It was dressed as the hunter from the Looney Toons cartoons; in his arms a hunting rifle was cradled. She didn't move for it, instead she reached up and pushed the plywood roof up and let the sun in.

"Knew it was too easy."

The light poured in and revealed the hair thin lengths of wire criss-crossing the room in a grid. She gently fingered one and pulled back sharply as blood wept slowly out of the small cut the razor wire had caused.

Victoria looked about the room, seeing no way to the gun without cutting the wire but that raised a thought in her head, "These bastards probably booby trapped the booby trap."

She backed out of the house and waded back of the house and walked down the "street."

The Director watched the lucky girl in the archaeology dig.

He smiled at the concept.

Some of the things on the island had been made with the purpose of being an interesting environment, such as the elements that were placed strategically around the island so that they'd be found for a tantalising duel.

The farm, suburbs and the bus depot, but the majority of the elements had existed back in the 60's, when the island was procured as one of the largest of the fifteen arenas for the Massacre, that were scattered all over the world.

The Director smiled, how they got hold of this entire island was to fake reports of an outbreak of a horrendous virus, by poisoning several of the original inhabitants. After the island was quarantined and a fifteen-mile embargo was set around it, they moved in.

Since its initial launch as the Massacre island, it had served as the host of thirteen contests, seeing the deaths of five hundred and seventy-two people.

The surveillance system was top of the range cameras along with seven aerial drones in circulation, three always in constant use while one was kept as a spare. The Director liked the fleet of smaller ones that could get in close.

He watched her from one of the bigger drones that was currently four hundred feet above her, circling.

He was annoyed that she'd spotted the razor wires but as she waded through the mud, he brought a small Dictaphone up and spoke into it, "Next time mine the archaeology dig site."

She'd escaped death thrice now.

Twice surviving bloody Mary and besting the rioter.

He looked up to the screen just to the top right of the one she was staring at, she'd began to get better odds and more money was being put on her.

"Maybe I should put in another call to Family Man." He stood, the room he was in swayed lightly beneath his feet, "No, I like you. You kill like you're meant to, unlike that bastard!" He pointed at the screen Teddy was on, he was in a kitchen looking through cupboards, "I wonder if you'll kill Teddy. God I fucking hope so. I just want that masked fuck to fucking end.

No one talks to me like that." He spat as he ranted to no one but his screens, but to him he was talking to her. "You're not like him. You're fucking honest, you do your part and so will that furry prick."

He sat back down on his leather chair, his little throne. He snatched up the earpiece and slid it into his ear, "Is lunch ready yet?"

"Yes sir. Would you like it sent up?"

"Yes and bring me something to drink. An actual drink at that."

He flicked the earpiece from his ear.

The Director knew he'd put the machine in motion to have Teddy killed, but it didn't stop him from sulking that Teddy had, in his eyes, turned soft and that just wasn't fun.

Dog sat the table in the fake dining room; he dwarfed both the table and the chair he was on.

He smiled to himself. He could still taste the chocolate that Teddy had given him. He'd been good and savoured it.

His head shot up.

A smell, a beautiful smell.

The door opened and Teddy strode in.

His jacket had been replaced by a pink apron and in both hands he held two plates with steam shimmering off of them.

He stopped beside the table, "Ah my giant friend, allow me to introduce you to your lunch." He laid the plate before Dog, "I present to you everything I could find in that kitchen. Toasted Veda, I am sorry there is no butter, sliced mature cheddar, grapes, maple cured Canadian bacon, and I may have found some ice cream in the freezer for after."

Dog's mouth watered and he moved to pick it up.

Teddy raised his hand and Dog stopped.

Teddy leaned in close to Dog and laid a napkin across the giant's lap and placed a knife and fork beside the plate, before walking (almost skipping) out of the room and returning with two glasses and a bottle of red wine.

He uncorked it and poured both himself and Dog a glass, before taking off his apron and sitting opposite Dog at the table.

Teddy set his napkin across his lap like he had for Dog, "Would you care to say grace?"

"P…p…pardon?"

"You say grace before you eat."

"Oh…Grace."

"Close enough." Teddy picked up the knife and fork and began to eat his food (sliding the food just in the small gap between his mask and his mouth).

Dog ate slowly, uncertainly using the knife and fork; he didn't want to seem rude in front of Teddy.

"So, if you don't mind me asking, do you have a name?" Teddy said between bites.

"Dog."

"No I mean a name."

"I used to…b…b…but I can't remember. I hurt my head." Dog felt the sadness at this, his owner would have called him stupid and hit him for even trying to think.

"How?"

"My owner put me in a box… when I was small."

"A box?"

"My daddy was a…he…he looked after people when they died. Put them in boxes for their family to see, then buried them."

Teddy's knuckles went white as he squeezed the handle of his fork, "Your 'owner' put you in one of those boxes."

"Yes. I was in there so long…my head hurt…couldn't breathe…didn't think so good when he let me back out. Spent a lot of time with doctor's after. Said my…" Dog became confused and rubbed his head, "…something was broken in my head because of it."

Teddy sat still for a long time, then his energy and psychotic nature returned with vigour and he sat forward, taking a drink from his wine (he'd procured a silly straw to avoid mask removal), "I believe you should have a name."

"But…"

"No buts. If it is not too much of me, may I give you name. I've thought of a good one." Teddy said boastfully.

Dog could only nod.

Teddy blew his chest out and placed his hand upon it, "Steinbeck."

"St..st..teinbeck?"

"Yes. It's the name of a novelist. He wrote a book I loved when I was younger, and you remind me of someone in it."

"Steinbeck." Dog said to himself.

"You don't like it do you?" Teddy said as if he was trying to apologise for an insult.

Dog looked up to Teddy with tears in his eyes and a smile across his face. "I am Steinbeck."

Teddy raised his glass, "To you, my friend, Steinbeck."

Steinbeck followed Teddy's example and raised his glass and Teddy clinked them.

They both drank.

Steinbeck spat his out.

"I don't like this." Steinbeck panicked, "I…I… I'm sorry."

Teddy shrugged and tossed his own glass over his shoulder allowing it to smash and spill against the wall, "Don't worry, no one likes to admit it but all wine tastes horrible."

Steinbeck smiled.

He felt safe.

With no warning, Teddy stood and held his hand out.

Steinbeck looked worried, "Did I do something?"

Teddy looked around, "No. I heard someone. Come on."

Steinbeck followed Teddy as they crept into the kitchen.

There were four men in the garden. Each of them scared Steinbeck.

Teddy took his hand, "Now Steinbeck. I'm going to have to do violent acts very soon. Will you be ok?"

"Do you want me to hurt them?"

Teddy stared back at him, "Only if you really

want to."

"I don't want to…"

"Then allow me." Teddy said squeezing the giant's hand.

He let go and snatched the meat cleaver that he'd used to slice the Veda, badly.

Teddy stepped out of the kitchen into the back garden and stood.

The men were facing the other way.

Teddy cleared his throat and they turned.

Three of them looked confused at the man with the Teddy bear head; one of them recognized him and instantly shit himself.

"Now gentlemen." Teddy began, "I am no longer playing. I bought myself and my friend inside out of the Massacre, so there does not need to be violence between us."

The man with the foulness in his trousers breathed out, "Oh thank God."

"But if you do not leave with haste, so that me and my friend can finish our lunch, I will have to kill you all in creatively painful ways."

One of the men who didn't know Teddy's

reputation stepped forward, a tall thin Portuguese man armed with an AK-47, "And why don't we just kill you both and take your food?"

The shamed man backed away, "Mr Teddy Sir, he does not speak for all of us."

The other two were starting to back away with the shamed man.

Teddy pointed the meat cleaver at the three of them while looking at the Portuguese man, "They are smart ones you've got there."

The Portuguese man spat on the ground directly hitting Teddy's shoe, "I've got a gun and you only have a knife."

"Oh this," Teddy said looking at the knife, "this is just to draw your eye away?"

"Away from what?"

Teddy answered by drawing the pistol from his hip with his free hand, and firing off one round that entered through the middle of the man's neck.

He collapsed holding his neck, coughing and spluttering.

Teddy took two steps forward and threw the cleaver, it embedded in the middle of the man's face and stood there.

Teddy holstered his pistol and looked at the other three, while wiping his shoe on the dead man's sleeve.

A moment that held the idea of possible violence.

One raised his weapon.

Teddy let loose a quick draw and fired off two shots.

Two of them fell dead.

The only one that was left was the shamed man.

"I'm sorry." He said almost in tears.

"I accept your apology." Teddy said before shooting him between the eyes.

Teddy stood quietly for a moment.

Steinbeck joined Teddy standing behind him.

"Was he going to hurt us?"

"He was speaking with intent to. Though looks like I've got myself a machine gun." Teddy said while picking up the AK-47.

"How long t... til we can go?"

  A ringing came from the house behind them, Teddy stood looking into the doorway, "I believe this phone call will tell us everything we need to know."

Chapter Eighteen: Courtesy call

Victoria heard ringing coming from a tent within the on-going trench.

She entered it and inside amongst camping supplies she found a thin satellite phone.

She answered it.

"Hello contestant. This is a courtesy call to tell you that you are now in the last twenty-five still alive on the island. There have been twenty fatalities."

Three of those killed had been by Victoria's hand. In all honesty she didn't care.

"Please keep this phone on your person from here on. We will be in touch with more updates as the Massacre continues. Thank you."

She bagged the phone.

Haru slid the phone into his back pocket as he climbed the peak in the middle of the island.

The cold air rushed over his bare chest and back, but it did not faze him.

He was making headway in his mission.

Gary looked down at the phone in his hands.

The clown was still by the coast; he was heading back to the town he'd woken up in.

He'd found the phone in a box with a speaker attached to it.

No one would have found it if it had not begun to ring.

He sighed knowing how many had died and threw the phone into the sea before stopping and turning around.

There was nothing there for him.

Teddy held the phone as the automated voice clicked off.

"Hello Teddy."

"Hello again."

"I've a boat en route, will be on the island by tomorrow morning."

"Mmm," Teddy made the obvious noise of hearing a lie, "I happen to know that you are offshore in that big luxury boat of yours. Let me guess, all the big spenders and runners are on board drinking and sexing it up while they watch all this fun on big TV's. So how come it's taking a day for us to get a boat?"

"We aren't sending the winner's barge or one of our guest's boats; we've had to procure one from Ireland and it took longer than thought to get it worked out."

"Fair enough. Where shall we be?"

"There is a lighthouse on the most South West point of the island. The boat will be there tomorrow morning at 8am."

"Why thank you. Now don't forget, I'm giving you exactly what I owe you when we see each other."

"Don't worry, I won't."

The line went dead and Teddy pocketed the phone into his front trouser pocket.

Teddy spun on his heal, "Dear Steinbeck, we have a bit of a hike ahead of us, but I know where we're going, I saw the light house he talks of when I was having a barbecue."

"What did you have at your b…ba…barbecue?"

Teddy shrugged, "A delicacy most would call an acquired taste. Now don't worry about that, we've still got that ice cream to eat before we go."

Victoria climbed out of the dig using the scaffolding on the other side.

She was covered in mud to her thighs. She strode across the grass for eight paces, wiping mud off her legs before stopping suddenly.

For some reason there was an American greyhound bus sitting in front of her.

She found herself staring at it for a good thirty seconds before stepping around it.

Behind it was a full bus depot.

She blinked at the sight.

It was as if someone had picked it up and just dropped it here from somewhere else.

There were only a few roads on the small island that she could see, so the mere fact that they were here completely boggled her mind.

"Yes, everything is for show," she thought, "but you have to have some sort of continuity of the norm."

She walked slowly into the depot, her boots

squelching quietly as she did.

Victoria counted twelve buses all in front of a surprisingly large building.

She froze though.

In the foyer of the building was a man tied to a chair.

His face was a pulped mess.

She crept forward and opened the door slowly, drawing her knife. The inside of the building had been completely decimated. Everything was smashed, cut, covered in graffiti or soiled in some way. The smell made her reel.

She got closer to the man in the chair; beside him was a duffel bag.

Victoria reached for it.

He grabbed her wrist.

She reacted quickly.

The knife was trained on his throat.

His eyes where wide but he was on the verge of death.

"Stop…" He said through broken teeth. "Nail…bomb…"

Victoria relaxed her arm and pulled it back, "Who did this?"

The man slumped in the chair, "The freak with…the…swastika…"

"Nazi?"

The man nodded tiredly, "He's close…fuckers…fast…."

"Thank you."

His eyes met hers, barely open, swollen and red; his bloodied mouth opened showing rows of shattered teeth.

"Run…"

She slid the knife into his bonds and began to cut them but froze when there was a thud from upstairs, and the most violent looking man in history kicked open a door and walked down unzipping his trousers.

"Guess who's awake and changed their mind about fucking!"

He froze when he saw her.

She ran out of the door.

Victoria darted between the greyhounds and pushed faster.

From behind, he screamed in rage and the door smashed open.

"I'm fucking coming for you!"

She was now being chased.

Chapter Nineteen: A good bit of ultra-violence

The Director erupted from his chair, "Finally!"

Before him on his screens he watched Marlow chasing Victoria with a shotgun through the bus depot.

The excited Director fingered his earpiece, "Finally someone has roused Marlow out of his nest. How long has he been torturing that contestant?"

"Better part of nineteen hours Sir."

"He's like a dog with a chew toy that one, see that the footage is edited down into a 'best of' packet for the snuff crowd."

"They might not be happy that he's not dead yet."

He shrugged, "The torture porn enthusiasts will love it." He rubbed his hands together, "Ok active odds with the bookies. Who is the favourite between these two?"

Victoria dived around a corner while shotgun pellets exploded into the bonnet behind her.

"Well overall the woman is actually getting better odds."

"She's a lucky one. I like her but I feel she needs someone more interesting than Marlow."

"Well Sir, right now, I believe she's brought a knife to a gun fight."

The Director laughed, "Oh but this will be fun. Marlow will run out of ammo at the rate he's firing it off. What was his personal weapon?"

"It was a…"

"Don't tell me. I want it to be a surprise. Is anyone else in combat?"

"No Sir."

"Then this is on all live feeds till it's over or until something more thrilling arises."

"Yes sir."

The blissful Director sat on the end of his chair, "And send someone up with some fucking popcorn!"

Victoria rolled under one of the buses while sucking a scream in as she rolled over her battered shoulder.

"Where the fuck are you?!"

Something near her exploded and rocked as

the psychopath fired off another round.

A boot fell beside her hiding place and she lashed out with her knife scoring the leather of the boot but not piercing.

His hand snatched out and grabbed her wrist dragging her out.

She allowed this and kicked him square in the face when she was free.

Something went crunch and a shifting of flesh and sinew moved under her boot.

"Fucking slag!" He screamed out swinging the barrel of the shotgun down across her ribs with a sickening thunk.

She tumbled backwards gasping as he raised it again like a club.

Victoria rolled away as the shotgun bounced off of the tarmac where she'd been.

She lunged forward and grabbed the barrel.

Marlow snarled and wrestled the gun under her chin, choking her against the greyhound bus behind her.

His breath, blood and spittle hit her as he screamed trying to crush her throat.

On reflex her knee shot out and caught him between his legs. He pulled back and she yanked the gun from his grasp, throwing it down the lane of buses.

The Nazi backed away from her holding his groin, his eyes ablaze with hatred and an anger that foretold horror.

She leaned against the bus catching her breath before lunging at him, bringing her fist across his already broken nose.

A crunch answered as he reacted, thrusting his fist into her gut.

She felt the air leave her as he grabbed her, holding her against the bus.
Panic hit before one simple thought entered her head, "Fuck it."

She head-butted him

The Director sat a gape as the two fighters rumbled, slamming each other off of the buses.

"Fuck me she's going to make us millions."

He watched as she got Marlow in an armlock and drove him straight back into the doors they'd emerged from.

The glass of the doors shattered as they both crashed through landing in a heap on the floor.

Victoria was atop of him grabbing him by the back of his head, slamming it off the concrete. She was lost in the violence until his elbow found her temple, and she found herself seeing stars as she fell onto the floor.

Her vision returned from the blackness to see Marlow stand and stagger towards his duffel bag.

From it he drew a straight razor.

He faced her, blood pouring down his panting face, "I'm going to fucking skin you!"

Victoria fought to get her legs beneath her while her hand gripped at the handle of her knife.

The Nazi went to make his move, but an arm shot out and grabbed him by the wrist.

Marlow screamed and turned to his victim and began to slash at him wildly with the razor, sending arcs of blood into the air.

Victoria didn't think.

She pushed up and drove the knife into his back.

Marlow howled in pain and spun.

Victoria felt the gentlest tug of her cheek before Marlow slammed his shoulder into her.

She fell but Marlow's victim still clutched at Marlow's arm with what feeble life was left in him.

Victoria stabbed wildly with her knife finding the soft flesh in Marlow's stomach and groin.

The psycho howled and groaned as he was pulled backward by his victim.

Slowly the dying psycho was pulled into his victim's lap and the beaten tortured wretch sank his broken teeth into the Nazi's neck.

Victoria pulled backward as she watched the man tear out the Nazi's throat spraying his foul blood across the room.

Marlow's eyes were wide but the fight was gone from him as he fell from his victim's lap and landed dead at his feet.

The victim sat back covered in his torturer's blood.

He sighed and looked at Victoria with his eyes

glazing over.

His only free hand touched his own cheek and as he lost everything he sighed, "I'm sorry…he caught you…"

He was dead and she was alone.

Victoria shook her head and felt light-headed.

She brought her hand to her face.

She felt it.

She began to scream but stopped, holding her mouth closed with a tight gripped hand.

Tears rolled over her knuckles as blood dripped through.

She couldn't stop it.

Victoria could taste dirty copper as blood choked the back of her throat.

Without thinking she walked into the back of the building in a calmness that was a horrid lie.

She found a bathroom and staggered over to the sink.

Dark blood pooled past her fingers and into the porcelain drain below.

She closed her eyes and let go.

Penelope's face came to her mind's eyes.

Happy and safe.

Far away.

Somewhere sunny.

She was beautiful.

The vision passed as Victoria stood looking into the mirror seeing her face.

A clean slice ran from the corner of her mouth straight to the middle of her cheek showing her blood covered teeth within, she'd been given half a Glasgow smile.

The tears stopped as a true calm hit her.

"Shit."

Chapter Twenty: White Shadow

Haru stared at the blackboard with some puzzlement. "Who is Teddy?" He asked no one as he read 'Teddy was here' across the board in chalk.

He pushed off of the desk he'd been sat on and began to continue his exploration of the building. The bottom classrooms showed nothing of interest, though he did find what seemed to be a child's drawing of a small boy beside a teddy bear in a blue suit. "Teddy again?"

Haru crept through the old school, the old building moaned in the wind. He knew this was a real building not like the town. It felt truly old.

He wondered where they were now.

All those children.

The phone buzzed in his back pocket and he answered. "Hello," the polite automated voice from earlier chimed in, "to help continue the progression of the Massacre, we would like to inform you that you and one or more contestants are within two hundred yards of each other. They have also received this message. Have a nice day."

Haru pocketed the phone and held the rifle that he'd lifted off of his first kill. Quietly he stepped up the stairs scanning the hall above as he moved.

He could feel them.

The first floor stretched out before him, the only sound was the wind tapping on the windows, echoing around him. In his chest his heart pounded slowly, like a blacksmith hammering steel, as he walked, he had his rifle trained before him.

He knew his fellow killer could see him.

Eyes burning into him from the unseen.

Something gleamed, Haru ducked and a thin throwing knife embedded into the wall above him. Rolling, he crashed into a classroom, kicking the door closed, only to hear the thunk of several knives smacking into the wood on the other side. Pulling the trigger, Haru returned the attack through the door, splintering off chunks as the rifle cracked.

Haru's hands shook, his ears rang and his heart only beat heavier.

"Fuck you." Haru calmly whispered to the

door.

He slowly stood, only to drag a chair over and prop it under the handle.

The gangster knew it was a futile gesture, but it helped him find his calm.

He stood very still and listened. Soft footfalls padded outside of the door and down the hall away from him.

He breathed out slowly and followed the footsteps in his mind.

Running down the hall.

Into the next classroom.

Window.

Haru turned to the wide window that crossed the entire room.

Too easy. He knew the killer would try to get inside.

"How?"

Slowly he looked up. Ceiling tiles.

He slowly backed into the corner as quietly as he could, and brought the automatic rifle he'd lifted off of the wannabe rapist up level with the ceiling.

Slowly his finger found the trigger and he held it gently.

This was what his hunter wanted; he knew this.

"I need to get out of here."

Haru crept to the window and opened it slowly before slipping out; he closed in behind him while he perched on the precariously small ledge.

He peered around the corner and looked into the classroom.

Complete stillness until one single tile fell with a horrid creature atop it.

Haru looked at the thing he knew to be a man.

Tall, lean, paper white skin and blood red eyes.

Haru ducked back around the corner to avoid the albino's gaze; he knew it would take him no time to discover his placement. Haru looked down; he was far too high to jump.

He had to climb.

Haru pulled himself onto the roof of the school and tried to collect his breath, but he knew that his fellow competitor would be on him within moments.

They were the only men in the building.

Neither running.

This was a slow duel.

Victoria could not feel the left side of her face.

The drug in the syringe she'd injected into herself had completely numbed the left of her face along with all notion of pain.

Slowly and methodically, she pierced the flesh of her cheek with the needle and pulled the thread through, thanking every deity in heaven and hell that she'd found the first aid kit hoarded by the Nazi psychopath.

In and out went the needle and slowly the two strips of flesh met again.

Victoria pulled out her knife and cut the lose thread and beheld her work.

It looked awful.

She knew that if she lived long enough that it would leave a disfiguring scar across her face.

She was thankful that Penelope would never

have to see her like this.

The thought of never seeing her daughter again killed her.

In the solitude of the bathroom, she allowed herself a moment to cry again.

Chapter twenty-one: It's a boy

Teddy walked through the woods with Steinbeck two steps behind him.

"Such a lovely day isn't it?" Teddy asked.

"Yes." Steinbeck said solemnly.

Teddy stopped and turned to his giant companion, "Is something the matter?"

"I woke up around here."

"Oh," Teddy looked around the woods, "why are you worried?"

"I don't want to go back there…"

"Do you think I'm taking you there?" Teddy said while stepping back to him, "I'm looking to have something to eat and I know there is somewhere around here that we can nab something nice."

"But didn't we just have lunch…and ice cream?"

"Yes, but I can hear your stomach and I'm hungry."

"You eat a lot for a little man."

Teddy patted his stomach, "Fast metabolism, think I get it from my mother."

Teddy began to walk and Steinbeck followed.

"What was she like?"

"Pardon?"

Steinbeck pushed his greasy hair back, "What was your m…m…mum like?"

"I don't know in all honesty. She died before I was born."

Steinbeck thought for a moment, "That doesn't make sense."

"I was what you'd call an emergency C-section. She was dead and I was still in her, so I was cut out."

"I'm s…sorry."

Teddy waved his hand, "It's not like I remember any of it, first few days of my life…though would probably explain a few things."

"How do you mean?"

"I've heard the rumours about me. Government experiment, ex special forces, a demon from hell…a bored postman. All wrong of course."

"You're no demon, you're Teddy." Steinbeck cheerfully replied.

"Thank you." Teddy stopped and looked at Steinbeck, "It just occurred to me no one knows really."

"Know...know… knows what?"

My horrible little origin. Would you like to hear it?"

"Ok."

"Now I warn you it really is not a nice story." Teddy said hands in the air as he walked.

"Only if you want to tell."

"Ok you twisted my arm, so my mother as you know died but she died during one of these."

"One of these?"

"Massacres. One from years ago. They used a town up in the arctic circle, one of those wonderful places where the days got messed up during winter and summer. Day and night can be stretched into months. So, she was taking part of this Massacre, forced into it I believe like yourself.

It took place over a sixty-eight hour day. The organisers had no idea she was pregnant. Probably because of her vest."

Teddy reached into his trouser pocket and pulled out his Star Trek wallet, he thumbed through it and pulled something, handing it to Steinbeck.

Steinbeck looked down.

It was a photograph.

Worn, discoloured, but the subject was clear to make out.

It was a young woman with bright ginger hair, brown eyes, a thin scar running over her nose from a bad break.

In the photo she was holding a large elephant gun and wore a large flak jacket.

"She's pr…pretty." Steinbeck said handing back the photo.

Teddy put it away, "Apparently I have her eyes…and habit of cannibalism."

"Habit of what?"

"She was in the games, of course back then there were no stringent rules and searching the players wasn't allowed, so no one looked under her big vest. Alas you can probably guess how this story goes. She was killed. Shot in the head.

Now the man who killed her took off her vest. I imagine looking for supplies... I hope so anyway. He finds this bump in her belly and for some reason he cut me out."

"That was ni…nice of him."

"I'd like to think so or I'd not be here."

"Not here to help me." Steinbeck said mournfully before happily adding, "But you're here."

"That I am. So, this man ends up winning the Massacre after killing every single person in that town, with little baby me strapped to his back. Now things get complicated. See some rules weren't in play, but some were. Since I'd been born there, they included me in the games. The organisers told him to kill me or kill himself. He blew his brains out. I feel quite humbled by that."

"He killed himself to sa..sa…sa…" Steinbeck stopped and started again Teddy waited, "to save you."

"That he did. He really didn't need to. Could've killed me and took the money, he'd certainly earned it and I don't believe I'd have held it against him."

"With you being a baby and all?"

"Yes, along with I'm not sure that at that age we really have any concept of anger or vengeance."

"Do you have the concept now?" asked Steinbeck, pronouncing concept slowly with every syllable, without stuttering, trying to impress Teddy.

"I'll let you know after I speak to your owner. Oh look a canoe!"

Teddy pointed to a canoe floating by itself in the middle of the lake.

He was easily amused.

Chapter twenty-two: Rats in a maze

Haru found himself in the school auditorium.

The large hall had many functions.

Six basketball nets lined the walls with different coloured tape marking out each of the activates that could be held there. Football, basketball, tennis, badminton, indoor hockey. One wall of the auditorium had bleachers pulled out.

His bare feet, raw from his travels felt good on the cold wood floor but every sound he made echoed through the great hall.

Each made him wince as though in pain.

He yearned for silence.

The other killer was quieter than him.

He knew this gave the albino the advantage, an advantage he wanted to remove.

Haru crossed the vast room and opened a storeroom, turning its light on; closing the door till it was open just a crack, then slid under the bleachers and sat on his haunches.

Slowly he shouldered his rifle and brought his

pistol onto his lap.

Haru hoped his brother was watching now, he was still in this game of death and had now found himself in a proper duel.

He could imagine his elder brother in the club surrounded by the others, all screaming at the screen for his victory.

This helped calm him.

Knowing he had supporters out there in the world.

But here on this island he only had himself.

Haru had not heard him but could not miss him, slowly almost spiderlike the albino descended from the ceiling from one thin cable.

He dropped to the floor with an unearthly silence and slowly strode towards the open door. His slender fingers slid into his pack and pulled two long blades, held between his knuckles and raised them slightly then stopped.

Haru knew he was spotted.

He fired his pistol as wood exploded before him.

As the smoke and debris cleared the albino was gone, but in the middle of the floor was blood.

Haru had wounded him.

He stood and slid out of the bleachers but something caught as he left them, causing his body to rock in agony.

Haru looked to his stomach.

One of the throwing knifes peered out.

Tit for tat.

The Director stood with his hand over his mouth watching the screens.

On one, Haru pulled the thin blade from his stomach, on another Moe limped down the hall hand over his thigh as crimson leaked from him.

He fingered the receiver in his ear, "Throw me an instant replay of that."

"Yes sir. Slow motion?"

"Of course."

Before him every screen showed one single image, he watched from a high angle as the shot fired out at the same time as the knife flew.

"Beautiful. Ok this could be a drawn out one, make sure this is continuously on the second network, while the primary broadcast gets regular updates."
"Yes sir."

He looked at the other cameras as they snapped back to individual players, "Give me an update of the proceedings."

"Well Sir the Yakuza representative and Moe are in the school, Teddy and Dog are heading towards town one, Victoria is in the bus depot and Gary is heading north. We've no accurate locations for Bora, Bloody Mary and somehow we've lost Family Man's group."

The Director sucked his teeth, "Let me know if anything arises."

"Yes Sir."

The line went dead.

He pushed his fingers through his hair and smiled, he knew exactly where Family Man and his people were. He'd had his personal staff put Family Man's group in a video black out so that no one would suspect foul play or game tampering.

He sat back into his chair.

The Director was beginning to enjoy himself again.

Gary sat atop of the hill in a sun lounger that he'd found by what looked to be burnt human remains.

He'd worked his way up here on a whim and he was deeply enjoying the view.

From here he could see the forest, the towns, the remains of the castle and what looked to be a farm to the very north, but what really amazed him was that when the weather cleared, he could see a ship out to sea.

A giant luxury yacht.

Gary pictured them there, the owners, the betters, the sponsors of the players all drinking and having fun, while their amusement tore each other limb from limb.

A speck caught his eye and as like before he saw a drone.

It was small.

Eight rotors supporting a small body and camera.

He knew it was watching him.

"Why is it watching me?"

"Hoping for something interesting I suppose." A voice calmly said from behind.

"I'm sure you're right." Gary replied turning to face the man he knew oh so well. "Have you been enjoying yourself Bora?"

The man he'd questioned was every inch a warrior. Every single inch of Bora's lean body was covered in the all-encompassing tattoo.

The pure white skeleton upon a crimson background.

Skeletal teeth separated as Bora smiled, "I'm yet to find a good fight yet."

"Is that why you've been looking for me?"

The Brazilian walked forward to stand beside him, to take in the view of the sea with the boat so far away, "I don't think either of us is getting to that boat my friend."

"Are we still friends?" questioned the clown.

"I caused evil upon you because of what you did to me, we're not friends anymore, but can we lie for a moment and forget the horrors we've caused each other?"

"I suppose it's the polite thing to do."

Bora sucked in breath and blew it out slowly, "Hell of a view though. I don't want to do this here. I don't wish to spoil up here more than the Teddy bear did."

Gary looked upon the burnt body, "What makes you think this was Teddy?"

"He played the music and stripped the flesh from the man's bones before burning him again. He truly is a wrong human."

"Well I'm sure that's high praise coming from you."

Bora smiled again, "We are all wrong here, just varying degrees."

Gary stood, leaving the comfort of the chair, "So if not here where then?"

Bora looked around before pointing to the North West, "There is a perfect spot just there. If we leave now, we can make it there for sundown."

Gary followed his gaze, "Well then old friend, lead the way."

Chapter Twenty-Three: A bloody horrible Massacre

Steinbeck walked behind Teddy as they entered the town.

Teddy stopped looking into the sky and stretched, "I believe we should make camp here my enormous buddy. Will be night soon."

Steinbeck looked up to see the sky had turned a pinkish hue, showing that dusk was approaching.

Teddy strode across and walked into a sports bar. He looked around, seeing shirts hanging from the walls, all for different sports from around the world including ice hockey, football, rugby, American football and cricket.

"I bet you anything that none of them are real teams Steinbeck."

Silence replied.

Teddy turned realising that he was alone in the bar.

"Steinbeck?"

He hurriedly ran towards the door.

"Steinbeck!"

Panic had taken him hard and he breathed hard behind his mask.

"Steinbeck!"

As sudden as the panic had hit it left.

Steinbeck stood in the door his hands clasped. The giant of a man, like a child who'd disobeyed a parent.

"I'm s…s…sorry."

Teddy walked to him and led him inside by taking his hand, "Its fine I was just worried. Where were you?"

"I found something for you." Steinbeck said sheepishly but with pride.

"Oh what?" Teddy asked genuinely intrigued.

Slowly Steinbeck opened his enormous hands and showed his prize.

"I…I…I think it looks like you."

Teddy gently picked up the trophy and looked at it.

It was a small teddy Bear wearing a blue nightshirt.

"Is this how you see me?" Teddy asked.

Steinbeck smiled with joy, "Yep. You're a teddy bear."

Teddy stood in silence not moving.

"Do you not like it?"

Teddy slowly looked up as a tear ran from under the mask, "Thank you."

"You are welcome."

A thump and a puff of pink.

Both looked confused briefly before Teddy looked down at the small toy, blood splattered across it.

He looked over Steinbeck then himself, only to see his blue sleeve beginning to be stained with his leaking crimson.

"Oh F-word."

Another silenced shot hit the pool table behind them as Steinbeck picked up the wounded Teddy and dove behind the bar.

Family Man looked through his binoculars.

"Shit Rose, you missed twice."

Rose hissed as she pumped another round into her rifle, "I hit him."

"I second that," called the Dane, "She clipped the masked bastard in the arm."

Family Man began to rise from their hiding spot across the street, "Well looks like we've lost the element of surprise."

Steinbeck tore the sleeve from Teddy looking at the punctured flesh, he was panicking.

A hand took hold of his hair and pulled him close, "I'm fine barely a flesh wound. Calm down."

Teddy slowly released Steinbeck's greasy locks, before turning the ruined sleeve into a bandage.

"Hello in there." A voice boomed over a megaphone, "Come on out and we'll make this quick."

Steinbeck held his knees close to his chest; he was breathing slowly, trying to calm himself.

"Listen big guy, we are only here for Teddy. You can run free and we'll get you later."

Steinbeck stopped panicking.

He stood and took hold of the railing around the bar, tearing it free, brandishing it like a club, "You hurt my Teddy and I'll fucking smash you!"

Teddy grabbed him by the arm and dragged him down as bullets crashed into the bottles behind the bar.

"Stop." Teddy said holding the giant down.

"But they want to hurt you!"

"I know, but you can make it to the boat."

"No!"

"Listen to me. There's most likely a back door to this place. Take it and run. I'll hold these blighters off."

Steinbeck took hold of Teddy's mask and looked him in the eye holes, "I'm not going."

Teddy sighed, "Well in that case, put the metal pipe down and take the machine gun."

Teddy rolled off of him and handed him the weapon.

Steinbeck took it.

"Do you know how to use it?"

"Yes."

Teddy pulled his pistol free, "Well Butch Cassidy and the Sundance Kid it is then."

"What's that?"

"It's a story where two men take on a group outnumbering them…it has a happy ending."

Family Man stood atop of the roof of the shop facing them, while looking into the bar as two of his group slowly approached the door.

A voice called out in a faux American accent, "Why you crazy, the fall will probably kill you!"

Family Man shook his head, "What?!"

With one confusing moment aside, Teddy and Steinbeck burst forth, guns blazing like the cowboys who had the happy ending.

The two at the door where riddled with bullets collapsing as the two screaming maniacs fired into their bodies.

"Open fire!"

Bullets crashed into the bar turning the room into a blender.

Steinbeck tipped the pool table on its side and ducked behind it as Teddy joined him. The green was torn apart but the old oak held.

Teddy cackled with laughter, "This is going better than expected."

"We will stop them then get the boat."

Teddy slapped his friend's shoulder, "Sure we will buddy, now let's kill them all."

Rose fired off rounds while the Dane let out short bursts from his machine gun.

Beneath them several of their compatriots fired what they had into the bar.

Family Man gritted his teeth, "Do not give the fuckers an inch!"

Teddy slowly looked through one of the pockets of the table and took aim with his pistol and fired.

Beside Family Man, Rose slumped as her brains sprayed across him.

"Fucking hell!"

He ducked while he snatched up her rifle, taking aim.

Steinbeck looked up at Teddy.

Teddy looked down at him, "I got one of them!"

He could tell Teddy was smiling beneath his mask.

That beautiful mask.

It killed Steinbeck to see it damaged.

In one horrible moment he saw it.

The entire side of Teddy's mask exploded as the high caliber bullet hit.

Family Man ducked behind the wall smiling, "Got the freak boys."

The Dane hooted in celebration before asking, "We let the big one go?"

"No." He looked over at his little weasel, "Chris, end him."

Steinbeck held Teddy's limp body in his arms sobbing.

The shooting stopped.

Jesus ran downstairs and picked up the end game weapon that had been stashed with the arsenal, that they'd been told about.

He aimed it into the bar across the street.

He fired the rocket launcher.

The Director sat truly astonished as the bar erupted in flames.

It took him a moment to react.

He'd done it.

He'd killed Teddy.

The cameras began to static out leaving white noise.

He fingered his ear, "What the hell is going on?!?"

"There was a camera router in there. The rocket has killed every camera within four hundred yards."

"Fucking hell!" He hung up and dialled.

It rang twice.

"Hello." Said Family Man.

"Is he dead?" asked the Director.

"The whole building is collapsing in on itself, we can't get anywhere near it."

"But is he dead?"

Family Man laughed, "Shot the freak in the head myself."

The Director smiled, "Enjoy the rest of the Massacre."

Darkness and pain.

Swirling disorientation.

Deafening wail of nothing.

Slowly consciousness returned.

Teddy's ears rang and his head pounded.

He reached up to his mask and felt.

The top right of it was gone.

He could feel hair, blood and bone.

"So I've been shot in the head." He said calmly to himself stating the fact openly.

"Teddy?"

Teddy sat up and looked around.

Smoke and crumbling rubble everywhere.

"Steinbeck?"

"Teddy?"

"Steinbeck!"

Teddy stood running, only to collapse as the head injury took its toll.

He sat on his hands and knees, eyes closed as his world spun.

A hand fell on his.

He opened his eyes.

What was left of Steinbeck looked back at him.

"No no no no no no."

Teddy tried to stop the bleeding, his hands slipping over the huge man's ruined body.

"Teddy…"

"It's fine, you're fine." Teddy lied taking his

friend's hand in his, "You are fine."

Steinbeck looked sad. "Your head is bleeding…"

"It's fine."

"There's a hole, I can see inside…"

"It's fine." Teddy tried to lift Steinbeck, "We've got to get you to the boat."

Teddy may have had strength that would terrify normal men, but he failed to lift his giant.

Teddy pulled off his jacket and began to tear it up, trying to bandage up as much as he could.

Too much blood.

Too much missing.

"You're fine." Teddy choked on the words as he lied to himself. "I'm getting you out of here; you can come home with me."

"With you?"

"Yes. I have a big house, lots of animals, cats mostly, you like cats, don't you? I'm sure you'd love them, Lady Maguire just had kittens, you can play with them. Would you like that?"

Steinbeck looked at Teddy calmly, "I can have

a kitten?”

Teddy was tying off the bandages and tourniquets, but it was a losing battle.

“You can have all the kittens, name them…” Teddy looked over Steinbeck before pulling off his own belt and tying it off where Steinbeck’s left leg disappeared beneath the knee, “There is this ginger one, I want to know what you’d call it.”

Silence.

“What would you call it?”

Silence.

“Steinbeck?”

“Your eyes are brown.”

“What?”

“I can see your eye…its brown.”

Teddy felt his mask, it had been blown away enough to show off one eye.

“You’re crying…”

Teddy sniffed hard, “I’m not.”

“Are you sad?”

"No I'm…I'm happy. You're coming with me." He squeezed Steinbeck's hand only to feel him squeeze back.

Steinbeck smiled closing his eyes.

"You…you are going to have a wee sleep and then we'll go to the boat."

"I am…t…tired."

Teddy stroked Steinbeck's hair, "Just think about the cats."

"The ginger one."

"Yeah?"

"I want to call him Teddy."

Steinbeck slowly let go of Teddy's hand.

Teddy didn't let go.

He held it tightly as Steinbeck's barrelled chest rose and fell slowly.

Even as the breath became laboured.

He held it when silence descended and the sun began to set.

Teddy slowly let go of his friend's hand and stood.

He walked slowly away trying not to let it in.

To repress it all.

Like all the other pain.

The horrors of his youth and the torture he'd endured.

All of the things he learned in the bad place where he'd learned to hurt people.

That was until he stood on something.

He lifted his foot only to see a small burnt teddy bear wearing a blue night shirt.

Then the screaming began, pained and broken.

For the first time in a very long time something truly horrifying happened.

Teddy was angry.

Chapter Twenty-four: Hunting the hunter

Haru staggered down the corridor, rifle in one hand, the other holding his stomach.

The blood trail had led him back up the stairs and across the first floor. Haru knew the albino was not moving fast but neither was he. He'd patched himself up the best he could, but he knew damage had been done.

A slither of silver flashed past him and clattered against the wall behind him.

Haru pulled the trigger as the rifle barked bullets down the hall.

He slumped in pain against the wall as the vibrations hit his stomach.

A way down the hall the slender frame of the albino limped down and around a corner out of sight.

"Come back here!"

Haru pushed off of the wall and followed the fresh trail of blood.

Gary walked beside Bora as day began to end

and night began.

"How many have you killed thus far?" Asked the clown.

"Only one…it was disappointing. You?"

"Same. A tweaking addict who was beginning to hit a really bad wall."

"Such a weak crowd. So many worthless ones."

"I don't know. There was one."

Bora sneered, "The Teddy? You think he'd be a good fight?"

"No." Gary shook his head, "But there was a woman."

"The addict?"

"No. I fished her out of the ocean."

"Why not let her drown?"

Gary shrugged, "I am here to kill you. The addict was self-defence."

Bora's brow furrowed, "That doesn't explain why you didn't let her drown."

"Just because neither of us will survive this island doesn't mean I can't help here and there."

"Fair enough." Bora scratched his chin, "Do you think any of those who run this game know who we are really?"

Gary looked at him, "Do you think they'd let us participate if they did?"

"They let that Teddy in; he's won a few of these."

"Not as many as us."

"Nearly as many." Bora stopped. "We are here."

Before them was what looked to be ruins.

Half buried walls and a crumbling tower.

"Is it a church?" Gary asked.

"I think so. I think it looks quite beautiful myself."

Gary pulled out his small pack, "Dinner before we begin."

"Sounds divine."

Victoria washed her cheek, wincing as the drug began to let the bite of pain back in.

She gritted her teeth and held onto the rims of the sink. She breathed slowly before applying the bandage to her face.

Victoria looked into the mirror seeing herself.

Battered, bruised, scared and tired.

But not broken.

She pulled her jacket back on, raided the Nazi's nest for supplies, then finally went outside.

The sky was turning a deep blue as night hit.

Chapter Twenty- Five: Man of the hour

The victorious Director exited his private area wearing a navy-blue tuxedo and salmon shirt with a blue bow-tie.

The Producer was waiting for him, the older man did not look happy.

The Director smiled, "Oh what's the problem?"

"The execs are angry about how you are handling the talent."

"Teddy? Well unfortunately he isn't a problem anymore."

"Dead?"

"Yes. Family Man's group managed to get him."

"I wonder how that happened." The Producer did not say it as a question, "Enjoy your moment."

The Director turned back to him and gave a polite bow, "You always told me this was the best part."

He turned away and pushed through the door.

As he passed through the door, he could hear it

all.

He made his way through the ship and entered the ballroom.

It was laid out like a faux awards ceremony.

Circular tables surrounded with chairs all in front of a stage, with a podium with two screens on either side showing live feeds of the Massacre.

His guests where sitting around the tables all waiting for him.

He decided to make a grand entrance.

The music roused and they all began to clap and shout.

He smiled and shook hands as he approached the stage.

A pat on the back from the man he had nothing but contempt for.

Whispers in the ear from an investor.

One caress of his cock through his trousers by a woman he'd be remembering.

Slowly taking the stage, waving at the patrons and taking to the podium.

"So is everyone having a good time?"

The room exploded in a righteous applause and he drank it in.

"Oh good to know I'm doing such a fine job." His smile hurt but he didn't stop, "Now when I took the role as Director of the Massacre, I had ideas and plans. I like to think this year I succeeded beyond my wildest dreams."
Another round of applause.

He held his hand up trying to calm the patrons, "But I promise you this ladies and gentlemen, next year I've something special planned."

A hushed ooo's and ahh's came whispering through the air.

"I'll not spoil it but damn it's going to be big." He winked, "Though that's the future, let's talk about this year, shall we? It's official, this is the best received Massacre to date, we've raked in…well I can't go into figures but believe me it's beautiful."

A man cheered.

"One of our happy investors I see." He waved, "We are currently broadcasting to more countries than ever before. Our private live streams online have so many viewing our servers have crashed twice; we're making sure those down in IT are earning their pay-cheques."

Another laugh dances across the crowd.

"Alas this year we lost one of our greats."

Behind him the screens showed a picture of Teddy.

"I believe he was close to his fourth win but one man can only do so much. Allow me to take you through some of Teddy's greatest hits."

A shirtless gore covered Teddy danced across the screens brandishing a pick-axe in a mine.

"Who can forget the win of the '09 Massacre in which Teddy managed to end the mad king's bloody reign."

In the Video, Teddy tossed the pick-axe pick first into the head of a crowned man as he stood eight yards away.

A sombre round of applause from the patrons.

The video shifted to a woman strangling Teddy with a garrotte in what looked to be an offshore oil rig.

"Or the truly brilliant end of the 2015 games with this impressive move."

Teddy fired a harpoon gun into his own stomach only for it to puncture out of her back.

"Or my personal favourite."

The screens changed to Teddy hanging one handed out of the window of a tall building, holding onto the collar of another man.

Teddy slowly weighed the man down neck first out of a broken window.

The crowd erupted in a thunderous round of applause as a long sliver of glass punctured the man's jugular.

The Director soaked it in.

This was his moment.

Haru limped into the lecture theatre.

His rifle raised.

The pain was excruciating.

"Come on out…I'll make it clean." He sucked in his breath trying to stay upright.

A flash of white and he was on him.

Moe held the rifle and wrestled it silently with the screaming Haru.

Haru pulled it close and head butted the spectre.

He pulled up to shoot only for Moe to lash out and strike Haru's stomach.

Haru nearly collapsed from the pain as his gun was thrown across the room.

Nothing to show for this he thought.

He was going to disappoint his elder brother.

Moe pulled free two blades and lunged forward.

Haru did not feel them enter.

He couldn't breathe.

Moe's red eyes looked into Haru's, screaming silently for him to die.

Haru could feel his mouth fill with blood but he didn't break the albino's stare.

He willed Moe to keep his eyes on his.

So that he couldn't see the pistol.

Haru squeezed the trigger and fired into the albino's stomach.

Moe held onto Haru.

He fired over and over again until his hand lost grip of the gun and let go.

Everything became wrong as Haru fell, dragging Moe with him.

They tumbled down the stairs together only to land at the bottom beside one another.

Neither could move.

Haru could feel it ending.

Everything simply stopping.

He looked over to his foe.

He was staring back, not with anger, simply staring.

Both trying to breathe but failing.

Haru lay on his back and placed his hand over the Buddha on his chest, knowing somewhere far away his brother would be proud of him.

Somewhere far away his brother sat silently alone, staring at the screen watching.

He was already mourning.

Chapter Twenty- Six: Revenge

Gary finished his soup as Bora did the same. Neither spoke now. They were past the false pleasantries.

Gary removed his long coat and sword belt.

Drawing the blades, he held the Uchigatana and slid the Daisho into the scabbard across his back. He brought his hand to his face and with effort, he rubbed what little of the clown make up that was left, causing it to smudge leaving him a truly terrifying visage.

Bora stood before him holding both of his twin Kukri blades.

The fire burned beside them, causing their shadows to dance on the walls of the ruins.

Both men stood as the fire crackled and roared.

Then they moved.

Lightning speed and the metal met.

The sword and the blades clashed as both sword men danced between the attacks of the other.

Gary with both hands on his sword, he brought

the attack hard causing Bora to stagger and leap through the open wall into the darkness beyond.

The dead clown followed.

Knives swiped close but Gary rolled, dodging, coming to his knee as Bora chopped at him.

The blades screeched off of each other painfully as each fighter put their weight behind theirs.

They pushed off, backing away from each other, slowly side stepping, breathing heavily while their eyes bore into each other.

They rushed at each other swiping with their blades.

Metal met flesh.

Blood sprayed across the grass as one fell dead. The other looked upon his fallen enemy. Silence held the night until the victor looked down at his own wound, knowing that it would end him.

Chapter Twenty-Seven: Doubting Jesus

Jesus climbed out of the bus and looked out at the last base.

A farmhouse. Behind it a barn and beside it what seemed to be a solid acre of corn.

The definitive image of pulp Americana.

He shivered in the night's air before a hand clapped him on his shoulder, "Don't worry Chris we're nearing rapture."

The thin man nodded, following him into the farm, "So what now?"

Family Man smiled, "Well we make camp here. Then we wait for the call to say we're down to the last dozen. That's when our games begin."

Jesus scratched his pointy chin, "But what if one of the others tries something before then?"

Family Man looked at him angrily, "They aren't that stupid. We are the masters of our own destiny and one of us shall be the winner, if one of us turns now it will ruin that."

Jesus nodded, "Has he called again?"

Family Man shook his head, "Not since we capped the freak and his partner. Probably partying with the rest of them in their boat."

"Fucking degenerates." Jesus snarled.

"In your opinion. If you win things could be different. This time next year you might be over there with them with a woman sucking your cock while you watch the next massacre unfold."

Jesus shuddered, "Is that what you want?"

"I probably won't be watching but the idea of the company sounds fun."

Jesus swallowed shallowly, "Do you think I could win?"

"Well you were fast with that rocket launcher earlier. You're a smart creature, so I think you have as good as odds as the rest of us."

They entered the barn.

The vast space was taken up by a colossal combine harvester.

Family Man wrapped his knuckles off of the outside of it only to hear a hollow knock, "Fake like the rest of it."

"What about the bus?"

"Exception which proves the rule." A coy smile crossed the organised killer's face, "I do remember being told there was something in here."

He opened up the engines compartment and reached in.

"Another weapon?"

"Something better." He pulled free two bottles of champagne, "Couple of dozen bottles in there. I think tonight we celebrate before we start killing each other."

Jesus took one of the bottles, popping the cork before taking a slug of it, "Sounds good to me."

He swallowed his new found spite for the man.

Victoria walked through the darkness, her only companion being the constant pain shooting through her body. She knew that her body was close to simply failing. She'd gone further than she'd known she was capable of. Victoria was going to go further.

She had decided to head back to the dig site, loot the place for more supplies hopefully by getting past the booby-traps. Her pack startled her by letting out a ring. She reached in and found the phone.

Victoria answered.

"Hello," the automated voice began, "you and another contestant are within three hundred yards of each other. They have received this message. Good night and good luck."

Victoria shoved the phone back into her pack and dropped to the ground.

Someone was close.

From the grass line she couldn't see much, even though it had been a clear night and stars shined above her.

That was until a small figure entered her vision.

A thin woman wearing military fatigues with a shaven head.

Victoria thought of what to do, then she saw it.

The woman was carrying a sniper rifle.

Instantly her gut told her that this was the sniper who'd twice before failed to kill her.

Slowly she held her ill-gotten shotgun in her hand and began to creep, following her, too far to get off a good shot; it would only startle the woman who could beat her in distance.

The sniper looked to be hunting.

Victoria kept herself as close to the ground as possible, knowing that the sniper could have a bead on her in any moment.

The opening of the dig site was so close she could reach it.

A crack echoed around her and the ground beside her erupted, spraying her with dirt.

She dove into the dark pit.

Mary screamed upon seeing who it was, "Why won't you just fucking die!"

She jumped into the pit after her, only to hear a boom as muck and dirt exploded from the wall behind her. Mary flung herself to the wall of the pit.

Victoria sloshed through the now chest high water, trying not to fall in the almost pure blackness.

Mary slowly waded through the filth with her

rifle raised. She could hear the noises of movement ahead.

Victoria slid into one of the small, half submerged huts while she checked the shotgun.

Empty.

She cursed herself for not checking it after taking it from the Nazi.

"Shit."

She peered out into the darkness, only seeing the small silhouette of her hunter. Slowly she submerged under the water and swam out through the darkness, deeper into the pit.

The party was in full swing as Family Man's group began to celebrate their last night on earth.

Upstairs in the master bedroom, the North Korean woman and the Russian where having what they called "End of the world sex."

On the porch the Canadian and the Dane

roasted pork on a spit over a fire.

In the kitchen Family Man was drinking with the rest of them.

Jesus was there but he was not with them.

Not anymore.

They were all beneath him now. He'd hoped that they could have been his apostles, but now he knew he'd been mistaken.

That's why he cleared up the empty bottles and began to fill them with petrol from the barn and hide them in the pantry.

Jesus wanted an ace in the hole, and felt a dozen petrol bombs would do the trick.

Victoria waited.

Her pain was only getting worse.

Her fatigue was only growing.

Her will was the only thing strengthening.

Slowly, her hunter rounded the corner, rifle raised.

The hunter's eyes darted but were blind in the dark.

Victoria tightened her grip on the barrel of her spent shotgun.

Her moment was near.

Mary's eyes were keen and well trained but this was beyond her.

"Is this hell."

The void answered her call.

Beside from the water, Victoria exploded brandishing her shotgun.

Mary held up her rifle in defence, only for it to buckle under the weight of Victoria's strike and fall into the water below.

Victoria raised her club again, only Mary tackled her into the water.

Both rolled and fought beneath the murky blackness.

Together they surfaced, gasping for air, but still swinging for each other.

Mary caught Victoria with a right but only for Victoria to tag her back with a left.

Both circled each other.

Victoria's stitching in her cheek torn, causing blood to run down her cheek and neck.

Mary's left eye quickly swelling shut.

In the darkness, they tackled each other again, rolling in the water and into another hut.

Mary stood, water pouring down her face, only to be gob smacked.

A rifle, within reach.

She lunged her hands open for it, only for her to stop.

Mary could see the razor wire glistening in the moon light.

A thought punched through her mind with pure terror.

"No!"

Victoria was already on her, pushing her forward onto the wire.

Mary thrashed but it was too late.

She was pressed into the razor grid, slicing deeply.

Victoria fell back as Mary screamed fighting against the razor wire, slowly pulling it from its housing.

Victoria remembered the booby trap and began to run as fast as she could.

Mary spun, wrapping herself in the slicing razor mesh as it pulled free the pins for the explosives.

Victoria didn't hear it.

She didn't feel it.

The world was black as the force hit her.

Before she hit the ground.

Her eyes opened in a panic to see she'd been flung clear of the pit and had landed on the ground above. Her mind reeled in shock before mercifully, she lost consciousness.

Chapter Twenty-Eight

A BLOODY GOOD MASSACRE

Family Man smiled.

Soon he'd get to win it his way, one way or another.

He drank heavily from his bottle, while his new friends celebrated their freedom.

Above him the classical music rained down.

The North Korean woman strode down with an exhausted Russian following her.

Family Man smiled at them, "You left the music on."

The Canadian and the Dane hummed away with the music as they ate their meals on the porch. As the record upstairs ended one song and began another, they heard the engine of the bus start.

The Dane looked over to his partner, "Thought we weren't moving it again?"

This thought was broken by Beethoven's Ode to Joy beginning to rise to crescendo, and for the bus to burst from the corn field heading straight for them at full speed.

The Family Man was halfway up the stairs when he felt the hit, the whole house shook as something crashed into it. He fell to his knees as he heard the heavenly choir join with the song.

Jesus was in the pantry stuffing rags into the bottles when one of the walls partially collapsed and he staggered out into the kitchen.

"What happened?"

The Russian looked at him, "I don't know."

Jesus was pushed out of the way by the North Korean woman, "We're under attack you idiots!"

"Who by?" Jesus said, while scurrying for a lighter for his petrol bombs.

He was answered by the door behind them being kicked in.

"Oh, that would be me!" Teddy cackled, while raising his machine gun, blowing away the two lovers.

Jesus screamed and hurried into the living room with the masked psychopath following. Jesus crashed into the man from Johannesburg and threw him into the thrashing maw that was Teddy, only to be cut in half by the answering machine gun.

"Oy you in the pink, stop being a spoil sport and stay still long enough for me to shoot you!" Teddy called from behind, while stepping over the temporary stop gap.

Teddy dropped the spent gun and pulled his pistol free, while he hunted for the pink coloured coward.

A thwack echoed out and Teddy reeled, feeling something hit his shoulder.

He turned to see an arrow sticking from it and an Indian woman loading a crossbow.

"Tut tut."

Teddy lunged across the room snatching the now reloaded cross bow from her while head butting her, before firing the weapon at point blank range, nailing her to the ground by an arrow through her neck.

A crack as a shot echoed out and Teddy felt a

chunk of his thigh explode.

Teddy staggered backward and fired his pistol in the general direction, hoping to hit whoever had shot him.

He rolled over the sofa as two men entered the room.

"Did you hit him?" called a voice.

"I think I did." called another, uncertain.

"Oh don't worry, you hit me." Teddy stood, firing and catching his assailant right between the eyes.

The other was quicker, knocking Teddy's gun from his hand and driving a knife deep into Teddy's stomach.

Stabbing over and over.

Teddy's hand found the man's face and gouged an eye with an angry thumb. The scream and satisfying pop delighted Teddy to no end as the stabber collapsed, holding his ruined eye.

Teddy pushed him out of the way while pulling the knife from his gut.

He strode into the hallway, burying the knife into the head of the confused looking drunkard who waited for him.

Teddy let the body slump, before turning back into the room and throwing the knife into the screaming man's other eye, ending his pained existence.

Jesus fumbled with his bottle and the lighter.

The blasted thing would not light.

He began to pray.

Teddy, ignoring his injuries, strode through the house screaming bloody murder.

In the study, he found someone, unfortunately they were waiting and opened fire with a small machine pistol.

Bullets tore into Teddy, pushing him out of the room.

"That's right mother fucker!" The man said giving chase.

Only to run straight into Teddy, who'd taken the bullets with inhuman indifference.

Teddy grabbed him by the throat and pushed him against the wall, pulling the machine pistol from his grip.

He pointed it at the man's face.

The terrified man screamed, "I'm sorry!"

Teddy shook his head, "Oh it's too late for that." And emptied the clip into his face, turning the handsome form into a hollow grotesque pulp.

Teddy dropped the gun and swayed.

He was starting to notice the near fatal injuries and blood loss were becoming a hindrance.

"Oh bother."

A floorboard squeaked.

Teddy spun and reached out, knocking something away from his face.

Family Man pulled the double barrelled shotgun's trigger, emptying a barrel into Teddy's left hand.

Teddy looked down at what was left of his hand in mild disdain.

Thumb, forefinger, half of his middle finger remained, though the rest was missing in a bloody mess.

Family Man raised the gun, but Teddy

slammed his fully working fist into the man's face shattering his glasses.

Family Man fell to the stairs and Teddy climbed atop of him grabbing his head with his hand and a half.

Teddy screamed as he began to slam Family Man's face into the stair with a sickening crunch, only to follow it up with another and another.

Jesus wept while clicking the lighter only for it to spark and ignite the rag. He ran from the kitchen into the hall only to stop in his tracks.

The devil was slamming the completely crushed face of his disciple into a broken stair over and over while screaming.

His disciple fought back, pushing the devil against the wall, screaming back at him.

"I am the way the truth and the light!" screamed Jesus throwing the petrol bomb.

The stairs engulfed in flames.

The devil screamed like a demon and fell into the flames, flailing, being dragged by the disciple as the disciple clutched at his shotgun.

Jesus ran from the farm as the devil was pulled to hell.

Behind him the farmhouse erupted in flames.

Chapter Twenty-Nine: Finish in sight

Victoria awoke in agony. She had broken bones and pummelled flesh. Her body was nearly done. She could only hear out of her right ear, while in her vision, white spots danced.

But she was alive.

Slowly she rose, leaving the smoking pit.

The sun was beginning to rise on the final day.

Victoria began to walk.

She was not sure for how long she travelled, or in what direction.

Only when she came across the stone wall did she stop.

She touched it thinking it was the castle but her mind corrected her. That was on the other side of the island.

She could smell smoke though.

The damaged woman stumbled around it to see a burnt out camp fire.

She saw it.

Gary's coat and his sword belt.

She picked up the coat and walked further.

A sound picked in her ear and she followed it.

It was digging.

She turned the corner while pulling her knife free.

Ahead of her was a figure placing soil with their bare hands.

"Hello." Her voice croaked weakly from her throat.

The figure turned.

Victoria did not recognise the tattooed man.

"Where is Gary?"

The man slumped onto his knees, "I just buried him."

She pushed off of the wall holding her knife out, "You killed him…"

"Yes." The man seemed pained, "But he killed me."

"How?"

"Poison on his short sword." He brought

Gary's sword and laid it on his lap.

"Are you Bora?"
He nodded.

"You got what you deserved." She began to walk away.

Bora sneered, "You think you know him…"

Victoria turned to him, "He told me what you did."

"Did he tell you what he did?"

She shook her head, "He said you killed his wife and daughter."

"His reason for revenge…but what I did was my own revenge for his worse act."

Victoria swayed on her feet, "What did he do?"

Bora looked at her, "Were you his friend?"

Victoria swallowed dryly, "Yes."

"I'll never tell you." Bora collapsed onto his hands, "If you saw him as a good man, why should I ruin that for you?"

Victoria walked closer, "How long have you got?"

"Don't worry about me…I'll take care of myself. I think you're nearly the winner. I heard a lot of gunfire from the North earlier. Sounded heavy." Bora breathed shallowly as he held the long sword in his hand, "I'd rather do this alone if you don't mind."
Victoria nodded and without a word left, continuing on her long walk to nowhere.

The Director entered his private room, half-drunk from booze and sex and turned on his screens.

He stopped, seeing the carnage at the farm.

He fingered his earpiece, "The fuck did I miss?!?"

"Well Sir…Teddy attacked Family Man's group."

The Director stood as if he'd been slapped in the face, "How? He was dead!"

"He survived."

"You have three seconds to tell me something good or you are fucking fired!"

"We are down to our last two players and…"

"And?"

"And we believe Teddy died in the fire at the farm."

"Well send the barge out, and after it's done, I want fucking confirmation of the fucker's death."

Victoria stopped as she could hear ringing from the phone in her pack.

She answered it.

"Hello. Congratulations you are one of the final two. Please head to the most North West part of the island. Thank you."

Victoria dropped the phone and began walking again.

After another excruciating length of limping, something caught her eye.

Something spinning off into the sky.

A firework exploded.

She crested the rise to see a huge barge sitting on the beach. Fireworks were launching off into the sky. She stepped onto the barge as it shifted on the wave. A giant screen flicked on and she could see herself from one of the cameras hidden on the barge.

The figure was not her she thought.

How could it be?

Thin, dirty, covered in blood, barely clothed by the ragged remnants of her apparel, only her jacket being in any reasonable state, cheek barely held together with stitching and ruined bandages.

She swayed not knowing what to do.

Her figure was not the only one on the screen.

Slowly she turned to face Jesus.

He held a small pistol in his shaking hand aimed straight at her face.

Victoria didn't move, if she did, she'd collapse.

He was smiling, "I'm going to live."

"No…" She croaked pulling forth her knife, "I'm not fucking dying here. Not now."

Jesus stepped back, but kept the shaking gun pointed at her, "I have a gun."

Victoria held her knife still in her hand, "I came here prepared to die but after everything I've been through, I've changed my fucking mind."

The smile disappeared and his hand stopped shaking, "You are a false prophet."

"What?" Victoria asked.

"I am the Shepherd. I will save the world. Behold your Lord and Saviour."

Victoria took a moment to acknowledge this, "Do you know what, you are actually the craziest cunt I've met here."

"Shut up!" Jesus spat angrily, "You are my last test, I will end you!"

"Mate, I think at this point, I'm just too angry to die."

Jesus tightened his finger on the trigger.

A trigger was pulled.

Victoria flinched, but stood wide eyed as Jesus was carried across the barge in a storm of sudden blood and violence, before he came to a rolling stop.

Jesus was moaning as he held the side of his body, bloody and smouldering.

The shooter slowly walked to Jesus and kicked him onto his back.

As Jesus looked his murderer in the eyes he began to scream in pure terror.

The shotgun barrel came to the bottom of Jesus's chin and he leaned in to look into his eyes.

"He wasn't playing anymore!"

Teddy pulled the trigger.

Victoria watched as Jesus's headless corpse twitched.

His killer slowly stood, and threw away the gun.

He was a man in a ruined suit, wearing a mask that covered half of his head, a lot of him was burnt, cut, bleeding, chunks of flesh missing from his body and what remained of his left hand seemed to be held together by a ruined neck tie.

The undamaged part of the head turned, and she could see the Teddy bear.

She didn't move.

Teddy walked towards her and held his hand out.

"Congratulations."

"What?"

"You won."

Music erupted around them as Queen's *we are the champions* played and more fireworks where launched into the sky.

Victoria looked dumbfounded at the anarchy around her.

She'd won.
Victoria's strength left her as she collapsed to the floor.

"Come here." Teddy said while holding out his uninjured hand.

She grabbed it with her uninjured hand.

"How?"

Teddy's eye caught hers, "I'm not playing any more…bought myself out. So, by default you win…your watch is broken by the way"

Victoria pushed off of him and limped away, "But…"

Teddy clicked his fingers and pointed at her, "You were the girl in the castle, weren't you?"

"What?"

"You know, against the armoured guy." Teddy clapped his 'hands' together, "Loved the flame thrower."

She backed away slowly, "Now what?"

Teddy pointed over her shoulder, "That's for you."

Victoria looked around to see a boat pulling up to the barge.

"Usually there are doctors on it. You might want to have a wee check-up."

Victoria's vision blurred and she stumbled but did not fall.

Teddy took her hand and wrapped an arm around him and helped her toward the docking boat.

Men in green stood by the boat and took Victoria.

She turned to see Teddy walking back to the middle of the barge, "What about you?"

Teddy shrugged and pointed, "I think that foreboding black helicopter is for me."

Victoria was too weak to object to the men carrying her into the boat and laying her down on the stretcher.

She had a fractured skull; one perforated ear drum, broken nose, two broken ribs, a collapsing lung, slipped disc, cracked eye socket, ruined cheek, three broken fingers, second degree burns, nerve damage and had lost over two pints of blood.

Victoria slipped into unconsciousness as the men worked on saving her life.

Chapter Thirty: What is owed

Teddy stood on the hill overlooking the barge, waiting as the helicopter landed near him. As it set down eight armed men poured out, all dressed in black and armed with rifles.

Behind them walked the Director.

Teddy waved, "Good Morning."

The militia surrounded him and boxed him in.

The Director stood behind them smiling, "Good morning yourself."

Teddy looked up into the blue sky, "It is such a lovely day."

"So."

"So."

"We have a problem."

"Do we?"

"You are meant to be dead."

Teddy shook his head, "Well as you can see I'm all here," Teddy looked at his mangled hand, "well most of me." His head snapped around to one of the mercenaries, "Oh I just remembered there's an arrow in my shoulder, could one of you duckies be a dear and pull it out. It's annoying me."

The angry Director shook his head, "There is a problem with you being alive."
"No there isn't." Teddy chimed while attempting to tug the arrow out.

"Do explain."

"Well," Teddy said, while tugging the arrow free, "for one thing it's good for me…I'd not organised anyone to feed my animals, so they are probably very hungry right now. Two, you get me back for next year which will probably cheer all of your higher ups right up, and finally I can give you what I owe you."

The Director stepped back, his face turning sour, "I don't think that will be happening."

He turned slowly, looking at the yacht that was slowly pulling in closer.

"I'll find a new killer for them to love, to root for. You will be forgotten, and you'll never give me what you think you owe." The Director turned, "Now…"

The voice caught in his throat.

Teddy shrugged his shoulders, holding the

bloody arrow with eight fresh corpses laying around him, "I'm sorry I didn't catch any of that…they were looking at me funny."

Teddy slowly stepped over the dead men and walked towards the Director.

"Now to give you what I owe you."

He was paralysed by fear.

Teddy stood inches from him, "Turn around."

Slowly the Director turned around and felt Teddy's hand on his shoulder.

Tears began to run down his face as he felt something prick and drag on his back.

"Here you go."

"What?" The Director said, while turning around.

Teddy slid something into the front pocket of the Director's jacket.

"I owed you that. Have a nice day."

Teddy strode off towards the helicopter.

Slowly the Director pulled what seemed to be a piece of paper from his pocket.

*'I had such fun this year. I look forward
to seeing you next year. Lots of love to my*

biggest fan. Your friend.
Teddy xoxo'

The Director collapsed to his knees as he read
what Teddy owed him.

A simple autograph.

Teddy slowly walked towards the helicopter,
looking out to see the tiny boat carrying
Victoria.

He thought to himself.

Seeing her before him.

Broken, bruised, bleeding, scarred.

"I wonder if she's single."

As he sat on the helicopter seat, he reached
into his pocket and pulled it out. The small
burned teddy bear.

"You seem a bit distracted."

Teddy looked up to see the Producer staring at him.

"Been one of those days I guess," Teddy said as he looked back down at the bear, "how've you been?"

The old man shifted in the chair, "Been better. I see you gave my replacement a scare."

"I thought I gave him an autograph?"

"I don't think he likes you."

"Oh now that's just because I don't always make a good first impression. I'm sure new Director and I will be best of friends soon."

The Producer nodded over to Teddy, "I had an intern feed your animals."

"Thank you for remembering, I'd have felt horrible if they'd had gone hungry over my forgetfulness."

"No problem. Same thing I do every year."

Slowly the helicopter took off and Teddy began to plan his visit to Steinbeck's Brother.

Somewhere in the realm of sleep Victoria was

happy.

She was with Penelope.

That is all that matters to her right now.

Acknowledgments

I would like to take the time to thank those who helped me in writing this beautiful cathartic piece of fiction. Be it my friends Nadine and Jordana who both read over this through about six different drafts or Rube Greene who was the first person ever to draw a piece of fan art for Teddy.

A shout out to Emma Lindow who took the time to act as last-minute editor before publishing, couldn't have made my own self-imposed deadline without you. My second edition would not have been possible without the help of Adam Kelly, a close friend who acted as my second editor, many nights and calls fine tuning the book until it was ready to be re-released.

A thank you to my family who did their best not to annoy me while I knocked out the first draft of the story while being fueled by tea and a morbid imagination.

Thank those who had enough patience with me to listen as I rambled off some horrible thing that would happen to one of my characters or to the multitude of ideas that where just a tad too fucked up to make it to the final draft. Once again, my heart goes out to those who helped me through this and that this book is for them...whether they like it or not.

Regards,

David Scott

www.ingramcontent.com/pod-product-compliance
Lightning Source LLC
Chambersburg PA
CBHW070344200726
48294CB00003B/781